BRET HARTE
—*From a Portrait taken in 1872*

HOW SANTA CLAUS CAME TO SIMPSON'S BAR

And
Other Stories

BY

BRET HARTE

ILLUSTRATED

Fredonia Books
Amsterdam, The Netherlands

How Santa Claus Came to Simpson's Bar
And Other Stories

by
Bret Harte

ISBN: 1-4101-0075-8

Reprinted from the 1900 edition

Fredonia Books
Amsterdam, The Netherlands
http://www.fredoniabooks.com

CONTENTS.

CONTENTS

MRS. SKAGGS'S HUSBANDS.

THE sun was rising in the foot-hills. But for
an hour the black mass of Sierra eastward
of Angel's had been outlined with fire, and the
conventional morning had come two hours before
with the down coach from Placerville. The dry,
cold, dewless California night still lingered in the
long cañons and folded skirts of Table Mountain.
Even on the mountain road the air was still sharp,
and that urgent necessity for something to keep
out the chill, which sent the barkeeper sleepily
among his bottles and wineglasses at the station,
obtained all along the road.

Perhaps it might be said that the first stir of
life was in the bar-rooms. A few birds twittered
in the sycamores at the roadside, but long before
that glasses had clicked and bottles gurgled in the
saloon of the Mansion House. This was still lit
by a dissipated-looking hanging-lamp, which was
evidently the worse for having been up all night,
and bore a singular resemblance to a faded reveller
of Angel's, who even then sputtered and flickered
in *his* socket in an arm-chair below it, — a resem-

blance so plain that when the first level sunbeam pierced the window-pane, the barkeeper, moved by a sentiment of consistency and compassion, put them both out together.

Then the sun came up haughtily. When it had passed the eastern ridge it began, after its habit, to lord it over Angel's, sending the thermometer up twenty degrees in as many minutes, driving the mules to the sparse shade of corrals and fences, making the red dust incandescent, and renewing its old imperious aggression on the spiked bosses of the convex shield of pines that defended Table Mountain. Thither by nine o'clock all coolness had retreated, and the "outsides" of the up stage plunged their hot faces in its aromatic shadows as in water.

It was the custom of the driver of the Wingdam coach to whip up his horses and enter Angel's at that remarkable pace which the woodcuts in the hotel bar-room represented to credulous humanity as the usual rate of speed of that conveyance. At such times the habitual expression of disdainful reticence and lazy official severity which he wore on the box became intensified as the loungers gathered about the vehicle, and only the boldest ventured to address him. It was the Hon. Judge Beeswinger, Member of Assembly, who to-day presumed, perhaps rashly, on the strength of his official position.

"Any political news from below, Bill?" he asked, as the latter slowly descended from his lofty perch, without, however, any perceptible coming down of mien or manner.

"Not much," said Bill, with deliberate gravity. "The President o' the United States hez n't bin hisself sens you refoosed that seat in the Cabinet. The ginral feelin' in perlitical circles is one o' regret."

Irony, even of this outrageous quality, was too common in Angel's to excite either a smile or a frown. Bill slowly entered the bar-room during a dry, dead silence, in which only a faint spirit of emulation survived.

"Ye did n't bring up that agint o' Rothschild's this trip?" asked the barkeeper, slowly, by way of vague contribution to the prevailing tone of conversation.

"No," responded Bill, with thoughtful exactitude. "He said he could n't look inter that claim o' Johnson's without first consultin' the Bank o' England."

The Mr. Johnson here alluded to being present as the faded reveller the barkeeper had lately put out, and as the alleged claim notoriously possessed no attractions whatever to capitalists, expectation naturally looked to him for some response to this evident challenge. He did so by simply stating that he would "take sugar" in his, and by walking unsteadily toward the bar, as if accepting a festive invitation. To the credit of Bill be it recorded that he did not attempt to correct the mistake, but gravely touched glasses with him, and after saying "Here's another nail in your coffin," — a cheerful sentiment, to which "And the hair all off your head," was playfully added by the others, — he threw off his liquor with a single dexterous movement of head and elbow, and stood refreshed.

"Hello, old major!" said Bill, suddenly setting down his glass. "Are *you* there?"

It was a boy, who, becoming bashfully conscious that this epithet was addressed to him, retreated sideways to the doorway, where he stood beating his hat against the door-post with an assumption of indifference that his downcast but mirthful dark eyes and reddening cheek scarcely bore out. Perhaps it was owing to his size, perhaps it was to a certain cherubic outline of face and figure, perhaps to a peculiar trustfulness of expression, that he did not look half his age, which was really fourteen.

Everybody in Angel's knew the boy. Either under the venerable title bestowed by Bill, or as "Tom Islington," after his adopted father, his was a familiar presence in the settlement, and the theme of much local criticism and comment. His waywardness, indolence, and unaccountable amiability — a quality at once suspicious and gratuitous in a pioneer community like Angel's — had often been the subject of fierce discussion. A large and reputable majority believed him destined for the gallows; a minority not quite so reputable enjoyed his presence without troubling themselves much about his future; to one or two the evil predictions of the majority possessed neither novelty nor terror.

"Anything for me, Bill?" asked the boy, half mechanically, with the air of repeating some jocular formulary perfectly understood by Bill.

"Anythin' for you!" echoed Bill, with an overacted severity equally well understood by Tommy, — "anythin' for you? No! And it's my opinion there won't be anythin' for you ez long ez you hang around bar-rooms and spend your valooable time with loafers and bummers. Git!"

The reproof was accompanied by a suitable exaggeration of gesture (Bill had seized a decanter) before which the boy retreated still good-humoredly Bill followed him to the door. "Dern my skin, if he hez n't gone off with that bummer Johnson," he added, as he looked down the road.

"What's he expectin', Bill?" asked the barkeeper.

"A letter from his aunt. Reckon he 'll hev to take it out in expectin'. Likely they 're glad to get shut o' him."

"He's leadin' a shiftless, idle life here," interposed the Member of Assembly.

"Well," said Bill, who never allowed any one but himself to abuse his *protégé,* "seein' he ain't expectin' no offis from the hands of an enlightened constitooency, it *is* rayther a shiftless life." After delivering this Parthian arrow with a gratuitous twanging of the bow to indicate its offensive personality, Bill winked at the barkeeper, slowly resumed a pair of immense, bulgy buckskin gloves, which gave his fingers the appearance of being painfully sore and bandaged, strode to the door without looking at anybody, called out, "All aboard," with a perfunctory air of supreme indifference whether the invitation was heeded, remounted his box, and drove stolidly away.

Perhaps it was well that he did so, for the conversation at once assumed a disrespectful attitude toward Tom and his relatives. It was more than intimated that Tom's alleged aunt was none other than Tom's real mother, while it was also asserted that Tom's alleged uncle did not himself participate in this intimate relationship to the boy to an extent which the fastidious taste of Angel's deemed moral and necessary. Popular opinion also believed that Islington, the adopted father, who received a certain stipend ostensibly for the boy's support, retained it as a reward for his reticence regarding these facts. "He ain't ruinin' hisself by wastin' it on Tom," said the barkeeper, who

possibly possessed positive knowledge of much
of Islington's disbursements. But at this point
exhausted nature languished among some of the
debaters, and he turned from the frivolity of conversation to his severer professional duties.

It was also well that Bill's momentary attitude
of didactic propriety was not further excited by
the subsequent conduct of his *protégé*. For by
this time Tom, half supporting the unstable Johnson, who developed a tendency to occasionally dash
across the glaring road, but checked himself mid-
way each time, reached the corral which adjoined
the Mansion House. At its farther extremity was
a pump and horse-trough. Here, without a word
being spoken, but evidently in obedience to some
habitual custom, Tom led his companion. With
the boy's assistance, Johnson removed his coat and
neckcloth, turned back the collar of his shirt, and
gravely placed his head beneath the pump-spout.
With equal gravity and deliberation, Tom took his
place at the handle. For a few moments only the
splashing of water and regular strokes of the pump
broke the solemnly ludicrous silence. Then there
was a pause in which Johnson put his hands to
his dripping head, felt of it critically as if it be-
longed to somebody else, and raised his eyes to his
companion. "That ought to fetch *it*," said Tom,
in answer to the look. "Ef it don't," replied Johnson, doggedly, with an air of relieving himself of

all further responsibility in the matter, " it 's got to, thet 's all ! "

If " it " referred to some change in the physiognomy of Johnson, "it" had probably been "fetched" by the process just indicated. The head that went under the pump was large, and clothed with bushy, uncertain-colored hair; the face was flushed, puffy, and expressionless, the eyes injected and full. The head that came out from under the pump was of smaller size and different shape, the hair straight, dark, and sleek, the face pale and hollow-cheeked, the eyes bright and restless. In the haggard, nervous ascetic that rose from the horse-trough there was very little trace of the Bacchus that had bowed there a moment before. Familiar as Tom must have been with the spectacle, he could not help looking inquiringly at the trough, as if expecting to see some traces of the previous Johnson in its shallow depths.

A narrow strip of willow, alder, and buckeye — a mere dusty, ravelled fringe of the green mantle that swept the high shoulders of Table Mountain — lapped the edge of the corral. The silent pair were quick to avail themselves of even its scant shelter from the overpowering sun. They had not proceeded far, before Johnson, who was walking quite rapidly in advance, suddenly brought himself up, and turned to his companion with an interrogative " Eh ? "

"I did n't speak," said Tommy, quietly.

"Who said you spoke?" said Johnson, with a quick look of cunning. "In course you did n't speak, and I did n't speak, neither. Nobody spoke. Wot makes you think you spoke?" he continued, peering curiously into Tommy's eyes.

The smile which habitually shone there quickly vanished as the boy stepped quietly to his companion's side, and took his arm without a word.

"In course you did n't speak, Tommy," said Johnson, deprecatingly. "You ain't a boy to go for to play an ole soaker like me. That 's wot I like you for. Thet 's wot I seed in you from the first. I sez, 'Thet 'ere boy ain't goin' to play you, Johnson! You can go your whole pile on him, when you can't trust even a bar-keep.' Thet 's wot I said. Eh?"

This time Tommy prudently took no notice of the interrogation, and Johnson went on: "Ef I was to ask you another question, you would n't go to play me neither,—would you, Tommy?"

"No," said the boy.

"Ef I was to ask you," continued Johnson, without heeding the reply, but with a growing anxiety of eye and a nervous twitching of his lips,—"ef I was to ask you, fur instance, ef that was a jackass rabbit thet jest passed,—eh?—you 'd say it was or was not, ez the case may be. You would n't play the ole man on thet?"

"No," said Tommy, quietly, "it *was* a jackass rabbit."

"Ef I was to ask you," continued Johnson, "ef it wore, say, fur instance, a green hat with yaller ribbons, you would n't play me, and say it did, onless," — he added, with intensified cunning, — "onless it *did?*"

"No," said Tommy, "of course I would n't; but then, you see, *it did.*"

"It did?"

"It did!" repeated Tommy, stoutly; "a green hat with yellow ribbons — and — and — a red rosette."

"I did n't get to see the ros-ette," said Johnson, with slow and conscientious deliberation, yet with an evident sense of relief; "but that ain't sayin' it warn't there, you know. Eh?"

Tommy glanced quietly at his companion. There were great beads of perspiration on his ashen-gray forehead and on the ends of his lank hair; the hand which twitched spasmodically in his was cold and clammy, the other, which was free, had a vague, purposeless, jerky activity, as if attached to some deranged mechanism. Without any apparent concern in these phenomena, Tommy halted, and, seating himself on a log, motioned his companion to a place beside him. Johnson obeyed without a word. Slight as was the act, perhaps no other incident of their singular companionship indicated as completely the dominance of this careless, half-effeminate, but self-possessed boy over this doggedly self-willed, abnormally excited man.

"It ain't the square thing," said Johnson, after a pause, with a laugh that was neither mirthful nor musical, and frightened away a lizard that had been regarding the pair with breathless suspense, — "it ain't the square thing for jackass rabbits to wear hats, Tommy,— is it, eh?"

"Well," said Tommy, with unmoved composure, "sometimes they do and sometimes they don't. Animals are mighty queer." And here Tommy went off in an animated, but, I regret to say, utterly untruthful and untrustworthy account of the habits of California fauna, until he was interrupted by Johnson.

"And snakes, eh, Tommy?" said the man, with an abstracted air, gazing intently on the ground before him.

"And snakes," said Tommy; "but they don't bite,— at least not that kind you see. There!— don't move, Uncle Ben, don't move; they 're gone now. And it's about time you took your dose."

Johnson had hurriedly risen as if to leap upon the log, but Tommy had as quickly caught his arm with one hand while he drew a bottle from his pocket with the other. Johnson paused, and eyed the bottle. "Ef you say so, my boy," he faltered, as his fingers closed nervously around it ; " say ' when,' then." He raised the bottle to his lips and took a long draught, the boy regarding him critically. "When," said Tommy, suddenly. Johnson started, flushed, and returned the bottle quickly. But the color that had risen to his cheek stayed there, his eye grew less restless, and as they moved away again, the hand that rested on Tommy's shoulder was steadier.

Their way lay along the flank of Table Mountain, — a wandering trail through a tangled solitude that might have seemed virgin and unbroken but for a few oyster-cans, yeast-powder tins, and empty bottles that had been apparently stranded by the "first low wash" of pioneer waves. On the ragged trunk of an enormous pine hung a few tufts of gray hair caught from a passing grizzly, but in strange juxtaposition at its foot lay an empty bottle of incomparable bitters, — the *chef-d'œuvre* of a hygienic civilization, and blazoned with the arms of an all-healing republic. The head of a rattlesnake peered from a case that had contained tobacco, which was still brightly placarded with the high-colored effigy of a popular *danseuse*. And a little beyond this the soil was broken and fissured, there was a confused mass of roughly hewn timber, a straggling line of sluicing, a heap of gravel and dirt, a rude cabin, and the claim of Johnson.

Except for the rudest purposes of shelter from rain and cold, the cabin possessed but little advantage over the simple savagery of surrounding nature. It had all the practical directness of the habitation of some animal, without its comfort or picturesque quality; the very birds that haunted it for food must have felt their own superiority as architects. It was inconceivably dirty, even with its scant capacity for accretion; it was singularly stale, even in its newness and freshness of material. Unspeakably dreary as it was in shadow, the sunlight visited it in a blind, aching, purposeless way, as if despairing of mellowing its outlines or of even tanning it into color.

The claim worked by Johnson in his intervals of sobriety was represented by half a dozen rude openings in the mountain-side, with the heaped-up *débris* of rock and gravel before the mouth of each. They gave very little evidence of engineering skill or constructive purpose, or indeed showed anything but the vague, successively abandoned essays of their projector. To-day they served another purpose, for as the sun had heated the little cabin almost to the point of combustion, curling up the long dry shingles, and starting aromatic tears from the green pine beams, Tommy led Johnson into one of the larger openings, and with a sense of satisfaction threw himself panting upon its rocky floor. Here and there the grateful dampness was condensed in quiet pools of water, or in a monotonous and soothing drip from the rocks above. Without lay the staring sunlight, — colorless, clarified, intense.

For a few moments they lay resting on their elbows in blissful contemplation of the heat they had escaped. "Wot do you say," said Johnson, slowly, without looking at his companion, but abstractly addressing himself to the landscape beyond, — "wot do you say to two straight games fur one thousand dollars ?"

"Make it five thousand," replied Tommy, reflectively, also to the landscape, "and I 'm in."

"Wot do I owe you now ?" said Johnson, after a lengthened silence.

"One hundred and seventy-five thousand two hundred and fifty dollars," replied Tommy, with business-like gravity.

"Well," said Johnson, after a deliberation commensurate with the magnitude of the transaction, "ef you win, call it a hundred and eighty thousand, round. War 's the keerds ?"

They were in an old tin box in a crevice of a rock above his head. They were greasy and worn with service. Johnson dealt, albeit his right hand was still uncertain, — hovering, after dropping the cards, aimlessly about Tommy, and being only recalled by a strong nervous effort. Yet, notwithstanding this incapacity for even honest manipulation, Mr. Johnson covertly turned a knave from the bottom of the pack with such shameless inefficiency and gratuitous unskilfulness, that even Tommy was obliged to cough and look elsewhere to hide his embarrassment. Possibly for this reason the young gentleman was himself constrained, by way of correction, to add a valuable card to his own hand, over and above the number he legitimately held.

Nevertheless, the game was unexciting, and dragged listlessly. Johnson won. He recorded the fact and the amount with a stub of pencil and shaking fingers in wandering hieroglyphics all over a pocket diary. Then there was a long pause, when Johnson slowly drew something from his pocket, and held it up before his companion. It was apparently a dull red stone.

"Ef," said Johnson, slowly, with his old look of simple cunning, — "ef you happened to pick up sich a rock ez that, Tommy, what might you say it was?"

"Don't know," said Tommy.

"Might n't you say," continued Johnson, cautiously, "that it was gold, or silver?"

"Neither," said Tommy, promptly.

"Might n't you say it was quicksilver? Might n't you say that ef thar was a friend o' yourn ez knew war to go and turn out ten ton of it a day, and every ton worth two thousand dollars, that he had a soft thing, a very soft thing, — allowin', Tommy, that you used sich language, which you don't?"

"But," said the boy, coming to the point with great directness, "*do* you know where to get it? have you struck it, Uncle Ben?"

Johnson looked carefully around. "I hev, Tommy. Listen. I know whar thar's cartloads of it. But thar's only one other specimen — the mate to this yer — thet's above ground, and thet's in 'Frisco. Thar's an agint comin' up in a day or two to look into it. I sent for him. Eh?"

His bright, restless eyes were concentrated on Tommy's face now, but the boy showed neither surprise nor interest. Least of all did he betray any recollection of Bill's ironical and gratuitous corroboration of this part of the story.

"Nobody knows it," continued Johnson, in a nervous whisper, — "nobody knows it but you and the agint in 'Frisco. The boys workin' round yar passes by and sees the old man grubbin' away, and no signs o' color, not even rotten quartz; the boys loafin' round the Mansion House sees the old man lyin' round free in bar-rooms, and they laughs and sez, 'Played out,' and spects nothin'. Maybe ye think they spects suthin now, eh?" queried Johnson, suddenly, with a sharp look of suspicion.

Tommy looked up, shook his head, threw a stone at a passing rabbit, but did not reply.

"When I fust set eyes on you, Tommy," contin-

ued Johnson, apparently reassured, "the fust day
you kem and pumped for me, an entire stranger,
and hevin no call to do it, I sez, 'Johnson, Johnson,' sez I, 'yer 's a boy you kin trust. Yer 's a boy
that won't play you ; yer 's a chap that 's white
and square,' — white and square, Tommy : them 's
the very words I used."

He paused for a moment, and then went on in
a confidential whisper, " ' You want capital, Johnson,' sez I, ' to develop your resources, and you
want a pardner. Capital you can send for, but
your pardner, Johnson, — your pardner is right
yer. And his name, it is Tommy Islington.'
Them 's the very words I used."

He stopped and chafed his clammy hands upon
his knees. " It 's six months ago sens I made you
my pardner. Thar ain't a lick I 've struck sens
then, Tommy, thar ain't a han'ful o' yearth I 've
washed, thar ain't a shovelful o' rock I 've turned
over, but I tho't o' you. ' Share, and share alike,'
sez I. When I wrote to my agint, I wrote ekal
for my pardner, Tommy Islington, he hevin no
call to know ef the same was man or boy."

He had moved nearer the boy, and would perhaps have laid his hand caressingly upon him, but
even in his manifest affection there was a singular
element of awed restraint and even fear, — a suggestion of something withheld even his fullest confidences, a hopeless perception of some vague bar-

rier that never could be surmounted. He may
have been at times dimly conscious that, in the
eyes which Tommy raised to his, there was thor-
ough intellectual appreciation, critical good-humor,
even feminine softness, but nothing more. His
nervousness somewhat heightened by his embarrassment, he went on with an attempt at calmness
which his twitching white lips and unsteady fingers made pathetically grotesque. "Thar 's a bill
o' sale in my bunk, made out accordin' to law, of
an ekal ondivided half of the claim, and the consideration is two hundred and fifty thousand dollars,— gambling debts,— gambling debts from me
to you, Tommy,— you understand ? "— nothing
could exceed the intense cunning of his eye at
this moment,— "and then thar 's a will."

"A will ? " said Tommy, in amused surprise.

Johnson looked frightened.

"Eh ? " he said, hurriedly, "wot will ? Who
said anythin' 'bout a will, Tommy ? "

"Nobody," replied Tommy, with unblushing calm.

Johnson passed his hand over his cold forehead,
wrung the damp ends of his hair with his fingers,
and went on: "Times when I 'm took bad ez I
was to-day, the boys about yer sez — you sez,
maybe, Tommy — it 's whiskey. It ain't, Tommy.
It 's pizen,— quicksilver pizen. That 's what 's
the matter with me. I 'm salviated! Salviated
with merkery.

"I 've heerd o' it before," continued Johnson, appealing to the boy, "and ez a boy o' permiskus reading, I reckon you hev too. Them men as works in cinnabar sooner or later gets salviated. It's bound to fetch 'em some time. Salviated by merkery."

"What are you goin' to do for it?" asked Tommy.

"When the agint comes up, and I begins to realize on this yer mine," said Johnson, contemplatively, "I goes to New York. I sez to the barkeep' o' the hotel, 'Show me the biggest doctor here.' He shows me. I sez to him, 'Salviated by merkery, — a year's standin', — how much?' He sez, 'Five thousand dollars, and take two o' these pills at bedtime, and an ekil number o' powders at meals, and come back in a week.' And I goes back in a week, cured, and signs a certifikit to that effect."

Encouraged by a look of interest in Tommy's eye, he went on.

"So I gets cured. I goes to the barkeep', and I sez, 'Show me the biggest, fashionblest house thet's for sale yer.' And he sez, 'The biggest, nat'rally b'longs to John Jacob Astor.' And I sez, 'Show him,' and he shows him. And I sez, 'Wot might you ask for this yer house?' And he looks at me scornful, and sez, 'Go 'way, old man; you must be sick.' And I fetches him one over the left eye, and he apologizes, and I gives him his own price for the house. I stocks that house with mohogany furniture and pervisions, and thar we lives, — you and me, Tommy, you and me!"

The sun no longer shone upon the hillside. The shadows of the pines were beginning to creep over Johnson's claim, and the air within the cavern was growing chill. In the gathering darkness his eyes shone brightly as he went on: "Then thar comes a day when we gives a big spread. We invites govners, members o' Congress, gentlemen o' fashion, and the like. And among 'em I invites a Man as holds his head very high, a Man I once knew; but he does n't know I knows him, and he does n't remember me. And he comes and he sits opposite me, and I watches him. And he 's very airy, this Man, and very chipper, and he wipes his mouth with a white hankercher, and he smiles, and he ketches my eye. And he sez, 'A glass o' wine with you, Mr. Johnson'; and he fills his glass and I fills mine, and we rises. And I heaves that wine, glass and all, right into his damned grinnin' face. And he jumps for me, — for he is very game, this Man, very game, — but some on 'em grabs him, and he sez, 'Who be you?' And I sez, 'Skaggs! damn you, Skaggs! Look at me! Gimme back my wife and child, gimme back the money you stole, gimme back the good name you took away, gimme back the health you ruined, gimme back the last twelve years! Give 'em to me, damn you, quick, before I cuts your heart out!' And naterally, Tommy, he can't do it. And so I cuts his heart out, my boy; I cuts his heart out."

The purely animal fury of his eye suddenly changed again to cunning. "You think they hangs me for it, Tommy, but they don't. Not much, Tommy. I goes to the biggest lawyer there, and I says to him, 'Salviated by merkery,— you hear me, — salviated by merkery.' And he winks at me, and he goes to the judge, and he sez, 'This yer unfortnet man is n't responsible, — he 's been salviated by merkery.' And he brings witnesses; you comes, Tommy, and you sez ez how you 've seen me took bad afore; and the doctor, he comes, and he sez as how he 's seen me frightful; and the jury, without leavin' their seats, brings in a verdict o' justifiable insanity, — salviated by merkery."

In the excitement of his climax he had risen to his feet, but would have fallen had not Tommy caught him and led him into the open air. In this sharper light there was an odd change visible in his yellow-white face, — a change which caused Tommy to hurriedly support him, half leading, half dragging him toward the little cabin. When they had reached it, Tommy placed him on a rude "bunk," or shelf, and stood for a moment in anx-

ious contemplation of the tremor-stricken man before him. Then he said rapidly: "Listen, Uncle
Ben. I'm goin' to town — to town, you understand — for the doctor. You're not to get up
or move on any account until I return. Do you
hear?" Johnson nodded violently. "I'll be back
in two hours." In another moment he was gone.

For an hour Johnson kept his word. Then he
suddenly sat up, and began to gaze fixedly at a
corner of the cabin. From gazing at it he began
to smile, from smiling at it he began to talk, from
talking at it he began to scream, from screaming
he passed to cursing and sobbing wildly. Then
he lay quiet again.

He was so still that to merely human eyes he
might have seemed asleep or dead. But a squirrel, that, emboldened by the stillness, had entered
from the roof, stopped short upon a beam above
the bunk, for he saw that the man's foot was
slowly and cautiously moving toward the floor,
and that the man's eyes were as intent and watch-
ful as his own. Presently, still without a sound,
both feet were upon the floor. And then the
bunk creaked, and the squirrel whisked into the
eaves of the roof. When he peered forth again,
everything was quiet, and the man was gone.

An hour later two muleteers on the Placerville
Road passed a man with dishevelled hair, glaring,
bloodshot eyes, and clothes torn with bramble and

stained with the red dust of the mountain. They
pursued him, when he turned fiercely on the fore-
most, wrested a pistol from his grasp, and broke
away. Later still, when the sun had dropped behind Payne's Ridge, the underbrush on Deadwood
Slope crackled with a stealthy but continuous
tread. It must have been an animal whose dimly
outlined bulk, in the gathering darkness, showed
here and there in vague but incessant motion; it
could be nothing but an animal whose utterance
was at once so incoherent, monotonous, and unre-
mitting. Yet, when the sound came nearer, and
the chaparral was parted, it seemed to be a man,
and that man Johnson.

Above the baying of phantasmal hounds that
pressed him hard and drove him on, with never
rest or mercy; above the lashing of a spectral whip
that curled about his limbs, sang in his ears, and
continually stung him forward; above the outcries
of the unclean shapes that thronged about him, —
he could still distinguish one real sound, — the
rush and sweep of hurrying waters. The Stanislaus River! A thousand feet below him drove its
yellowing current. Through all the vacillations of
his unseated mind he had clung to one idea, — to
reach the river, to lave in it, to swim it if need be,
but to put it forever between him and the harry-
ing shapes, to drown forever in its turbid depths
the thronging spectres, to wash away in its yel-

low flood all stains and color of the past. And now he was leaping from boulder to boulder, from blackened stump to stump, from gnarled bush to bush, caught for a moment and withheld by clinging vines, or plunging downward into dusty hollows, until, rolling, dropping, sliding, and stumbling, he reached the river-bank, whereon he fell, rose, staggered forward, and fell again with outstretched arms upon a rock that breasted the swift current. And there he lay as dead.

A few stars came out hesitatingly above Deadwood Slope. A cold wind that had sprung up with the going down of the sun fanned them into momentary brightness, swept the heated flanks of the mountain, and ruffled the river. Where the fallen man lay there was a sharp curve in the stream, so that in the gathering shadows the rushing water seemed to leap out of the darkness and to vanish again. Decayed drift-wood, trunks of trees, fragments of broken sluicing, — the wash and waste of many a mile, — swept into sight a moment, and were gone. All of decay, wreck, and foulness gathered in the long circuit of miningcamp and settlement, all the dregs and refuse of a crude and wanton civilization, reappeared for an instant, and then were hurried away in the darkness and lost. No wonder that as the wind ruffled the yellow waters the waves seemed to lift their unclean hands toward the rock whereon the fallen man lay, as if eager to snatch him from it, too, and hurry him toward the sea.

It was very still. In the clear air a horn blown a mile away was heard distinctly. The jingling of a spur and a laugh on the highway over Payne's Ridge sounded clearly across the river. The rattling of harness and hoofs foretold for many minutes the approach of the Wingdam coach, that at last, with flashing lights, passed within a few feet of the rock. Then for an hour all again was quiet. Presently the moon, round and full, lifted herself above the serried ridge and looked down upon the river. At first the bared peak of Deadwood Hill gleamed white and skull-like. Then the shadows of Payne's Ridge cast on the slope slowly sank away, leaving the unshapely stumps, the dusty fissures, and clinging outcrop of Deadwood Slope to stand out in black and silver. Still stealing softly downward, the moonlight touched the bank and the rock, and then glittered brightly on the river. The rock was bare and the man was gone, but the river still hurried swiftly to the sea.

"Is there anything for me?" asked Tommy Islington, as, a week after, the stage drew up at the Mansion House, and Bill slowly entered the barroom. Bill did not reply, but, turning to a stranger who had entered with him, indicated with a jerk of his finger the boy. The stranger turned

with an air half of business, half of curiosity, and
looked critically at Tommy. "Is there anything
for me ?" repeated Tommy, a little confused at the
silence and scrutiny. Bill walked deliberately to
the bar, and, placing his back against it, faced
Tommy with a look of demure enjoyment.

"Ef," he remarked slowly, — "ef a hundred
thousand dollars down and half a million in per-
spektive is ennything, Major, THERE IS !"

MRS. SKAGGS'S HUSBANDS.

IT was characteristic of Angel's that the disappearance of Johnson, and the fact that he had left his entire property to Tommy, thrilled the community but slightly in comparison with the astounding discovery that he had anything to leave. The finding of a cinnabar lode at Angel's absorbed all collateral facts or subsequent details. Prospectors from adjoining camps thronged the settlement; the hillside for a mile on either side of Johnson's claim was staked out and pre-empted; trade received a sudden stimulus; and, in the excited rhetoric of the " Weekly Record," " a new era had broken upon Angel's." " On Thursday last," added that paper, " over five hundred dollars was taken in over the bar of the Mansion House."

Of the fate of Johnson there was little doubt. He had been last seen lying on a boulder on the river-bank by outside passengers of the Wingdam night coach, and when Finn of Robinson's Ferry admitted to have fired three shots from a revolver at a dark object struggling in the water near the ferry, which he " suspicioned " to be a bear, the question seemed to be settled. Whatever might have been the fallibility of his judgment, of the accuracy of his aim there could be no doubt. The general belief that Johnson, after possessing himself of the muleteer's pistol, could have run amuck, gave a certain retributive justice to this story, which rendered it acceptable to the camp.

It was also characteristic of Angel's that no feeling of envy or opposition to the good fortune of Tommy Islington prevailed there. That he was thoroughly cognizant, from the first, of Johnson's discovery, that his attentions to him were interested, calculating, and speculative was, however, the general belief of the majority, — a belief that, singularly enough, awakened the first feelings of genuine respect for Tommy ever shown by the camp. "He ain't no fool; Yuba Bill seed thet from the first," said the barkeeper. It was Yuba Bill who applied for the guardianship of Tommy after his accession to Johnson's claim, and on whose bonds the richest men of Calaveras were represented. It was Yuba Bill, also, when Tommy was sent East to finish his education, accompanied him to San Francisco, and, before parting with his charge on the steamer's deck, drew him aside, and said, "Ef at enny time you want enny money, Tommy, over and 'bove your 'lowance, you kin write; but ef you 'll take my advice," he added, with a sudden huskiness mitigating the severity of his voice, "you 'll forget every

derned ole spavined, string-halted bummer as you
ever met or knew at Angel's, — ev'ry one, Tommy,
— ev'ry one! And so — boy — take care of yourself — and — and — God bless ye, and pertikerly
d—n me for a first-class A 1 fool." It was
Yuba Bill, also, after this speech, glared savagely
around, walked down the crowded gang-plank
with a rigid and aggressive shoulder, picked a
quarrel with his cabman, and, after bundling that
functionary into his own vehicle, took the reins
himself, and drove furiously to his hotel. "It cost
me," said Bill, recounting the occurrence somewhat
later at Angel's, — "it cost me a matter o' twenty
dollars afore the jedge the next mornin'; but you
kin bet high thet I taught them 'Frisco chaps
suthin new about drivin'. I did n't make it lively
in Montgomery Street for about ten minutes, —
O no!"

And so by degrees the two original locaters of
the great Cinnabar Lode faded from the memory
of Angel's, and Calaveras knew them no more. In
five years their very names had been forgotten;
in seven the name of the town was changed; in
ten the town itself was transported bodily to the
hillside, and the chimney of the Union Smelting
Works by night flickered like a corpse-light over
the site of Johnson's cabin, and by day poisoned
the pure spices of the pines. Even the Mansion
House was dismantled, and the Wingdam stage

deserted the highway for a shorter cut by Quicksilver City. Only the bared crest of Deadwood Hill, as of old, sharply cut the clear blue sky, and at its base, as of old, the Stanislaus River, unwearied and unresting, babbled, whispered, and hurried away to the sea.

A midsummer's day was breaking lazily on the Atlantic. There was not wind enough to move the vapors in the foggy offing, but where the vague distance heaved against a violet sky there were dull red streaks that, growing brighter, presently painted out the stars. Soon the brown rocks of Greyport appeared faintly suffused, and then the whole ashen line of dead coast was kindled, and the lighthouse beacons went out one by one. And then a hundred sail, before invisible, started out of the vapory horizon, and pressed toward the shore. It was morning, indeed, and some of the best society in Greyport, having been up all night, were thinking it was time to go to bed.

For as the sky flashed brighter it fired the clustering red roofs of a picturesque house by the sands that had all that night, from open lattice and illuminated balcony, given light and music to the shore. It glittered on the broad crystal spaces of a great conservatory that looked upon an exquisite lawn, where all night long the blended odors of sea and shore had swooned under the summer

moon. But it wrought confusion among the
colored lamps on the long veranda, and startled
a group of ladies and gentlemen who had stepped
from the drawing-room window to gaze upon it.
It was so searching and sincere in its way, that, as
the carriage of the fairest Miss Gillyflower rolled
away, that peerless young woman, catching sight
of her face in the oval mirror, instantly pulled
down the blinds, and, nestling the whitest shoulders
in Greyport against the crimson cushions, went to
sleep.

"How haggard everybody is! Rose, dear, you
look almost intellectual," said Blanche Masterman.

"I hope not," said Rose, simply. "Sunrises are
very trying. Look how that pink regularly puts
out Mrs. Brown-Robinson, hair and all!"

"The angels," said the Count de Nugat, with a
polite gesture toward the sky, "must have find
these celestial combinations very bad for the *toi-
lette*."

"They 're safe in white, — except when they sit
for their pictures in Venice," said Blanche. "How
fresh Mr. Islington looks! It 's really uncomplimentary to us."

"I suppose the sun recognizes in me no rival,"
said the young man, demurely. "But," he added,
"I have lived much in the open air, and require
very little sleep."

"How delightful!" said Mrs. Brown-Robinson,

in a low, enthusiastic voice, and a manner that held
the glowing sentiment of sixteen and the practical
experiences of thirty-two in dangerous combination;
— "how perfectly delightful! What sunrises you
must have seen, and in such wild, romantic places!
How I envy you! My nephew was a classmate
of yours, and has often repeated to me those charming stories you tell of your adventures. Won't
you tell some now? Do! How you must tire of
us and this artificial life here, so frightfully artificial, you know" (in a confidential whisper); "and
then to think of the days when you roamed the
great West with the Indians, and the bisons, and
the grizzly bears! Of course, you have seen grizzly bears and bisons?"

"Of course he has, dear," said Blanche, a little
pettishly, throwing a cloak over her shoulders, and
seizing her *chaperon* by the arm; "his earliest in-
fancy was soothed by bisons, and he proudly points
to the grizzly bear as the playmate of his youth.
Come with me, and I'll tell you all about it. How
good it is of you," she added, *sotto voce*, to Islington,
as he stood by the carriage, — "how perfectly good
it is of you to be like those animals you tell us of,
and not know your full power. Think, with your
experiences and our credulity, what stories you
might tell! And you are going to walk? Good
night, then." A slim, gloved hand was frankly extended from the window, and the next moment the
carriage rolled away.

" Is n't Islington throwing away a chance there ? "
said Captain Merwin, on the veranda.

" Perhaps he could n't stand my lovely aunt's
superadded presence. But then, he 's the guest
of Blanche's father, and I dare say they see enough
of each other as it is."

" But is n't it a rather dangerous situation ? "

" For him, perhaps ; although he 's awfully
old, and very queer. For her, with an experience
that takes in all the available men in both hemi-
spheres, ending with Nugat over there, I should
say a man more or less would n't affect her much,
anyway. Of course," he laughed, " these are the
accents of bitterness. But that was last year."

Perhaps Islington did not overhear the speaker ;
perhaps, if he did, the criticism was not new. He
turned carelessly away, and sauntered out on the
road to the sea. Thence he strolled along the sands
toward the cliffs, where, meeting an impediment in
the shape of a garden wall, he leaped it with a certain
agile, boyish ease and experience, and struck across
an open lawn toward the rocks again. The best society of Greyport were not early risers, and the
spectacle of a trespasser in an evening dress excited only the criticism of grooms hanging about
the stables, or cleanly housemaids on the broad ve-
randas that in Greyport architecture dutifully gave
upon the sea. Only once, as he entered the boun-
daries of Cliffwood Lodge, the famous seat of

Renwyck Masterman, was he aware of suspicious
scrutiny; but a slouching figure that vanished
quickly in the lodge offered no opposition to his
progress.   Avoiding the pathway to the lodge, Islington kept along the rocks until, reaching a little
promontory and rustic pavilion, he sat down and
gazed upon the sea.

And presently an infinite peace stole upon him.
Except where the waves lapped lazily the crags
below, the vast expanse beyond seemed unbroken
by ripple, heaving only in broad ponderable sheets,
and rhythmically, as if still in sleep.   The air was
filled with a luminous haze that caught and held
the direct sunbeams.   In the deep calm that lay
upon the sea, it seemed to Islington that all the
tenderness of culture, magic of wealth, and spell
of refinement that for years had wrought upon
that favored shore had extended its gracious influence even here.   What a pampered and caressed
old ocean it was; cajoled, flattered, and *féted* where
it lay !   An odd recollection of the turbid Stanislaus hurrying by the ascetic pines, of the grim
outlines of Deadwood Hill, swam before his eyes,
and made the yellow green of the velvet lawn
and graceful foliage seem almost tropical by contrast.   And, looking up, a few yards distant he beheld a tall slip of a girl gazing upon the sea, —
Blanche Masterman.

She had plucked somewhere a large fan-shaped

leaf, which she held parasol-wise, shading the blond masses of her hair, and hiding her gray eyes. She had changed her festal dress, with its amplitude of flounce and train, for a closely fitting half-antique habit whose scant outlines would have been trying to limbs less shapely, but which prettily accented the graceful curves and sweeping lines of this Greyport goddess. As Islington rose, she came toward him with a frankly outstretched hand and unconstrained manner. Had she observed him first? I don't know.

They sat down together on a rustic seat, Miss Blanche facing the sea, and shading her eyes with the leaf.

"I don't really know how long I have been sitting here," said Islington, "or whether I have not been actually asleep and dreaming. It seemed too lovely a morning to go to bed. But you?"

From behind the leaf, it appeared that Miss Blanche, on retiring, had been pursued by a hideous winged bug which defied the efforts of herself and maid to dislodge. Odin, the Spitz dog, had insisted upon scratching at the door. And it made her eyes red to sleep in the morning. And she had an early call to make. And the sea looked lovely.

"I'm glad to find you here, whatever be the cause," said Islington, with his old directness. "To-day, as you know, is my last day in Greyport, and it is much pleasanter to say good by under this blue sky than even beneath your father's wonderful frescos yonder I want to remember you, too, as part of this pleasant prospect which belongs to us all, rather than recall you in anybody's particular setting."

"I know," said Blanche, with equal directness, "that houses are one of the defects of our civilization; but I don't think I ever heard the idea as elegantly expressed before. Where do you go?"

"I don't know yet. I have several plans. I may go to South America and become president of one of the republics, — I am not particular which. I am rich, but in that part of America which lies outside of Greyport it is necessary for every man to have some work. My friends think I should have some great aim in life, with a capital A. But I was born a vagabond, and a vagabond I shall probably die."

"I don't know anybody in South America," said Blanche, languidly. "There were two girls here last season, but they did n't wear stays in the house, and their white frocks never were properly done up. If you go to South America, you must write to me."

"I will. Can you tell me the name of this flower which I found in your greenhouse. It looks much like a California blossom."

"Perhaps it is. Father bought it of a half-crazy

old man who came here one day. Do you know him?"

Islington laughed. "I am afraid not. But let me present this in a less business-like fashion."

"Thank you. Remind me to give you one in return before you go, — or will you choose yourself?"

They had both risen as by a common instinct.

"Good by."

The cool flower-like hand lay in his for an instant.

"Will you oblige me by putting aside that leaf a moment before I go?"

"But my eyes are red, and I look like a perfect fright."

Yet, after a long pause, the leaf fluttered down, and a pair of very beautiful but withal very clear and critical eyes met his. Islington was constrained to look away. When he turned again, she was gone.

"Mister Hislington, — sir!"

It was Chalker, the English groom, out of breath with running.

"Seein' you alone, sir, — beg your pardon, sir, — but there's a person — "

"A person! what the devil do you mean? Speak English — no, damn it, I mean don't," said Islington, snappishly.

"I sed a person, sir. Beg pardon — no offence — but not a gent, sir. In the lib'ry."

A little amused even through the utter dissatisfaction with himself and vague loneliness that had suddenly come upon him, Islington, as he walked toward the lodge, asked, " Why is n't he a gent ?

" No gent — beggin' your pardin, sir — 'ud guy a man in sarvis, sir. Takes me 'ands so, sir, as I sits in the rumble at the gate, and puts 'em downd so, sir, and sez, ' Put 'em in your pocket, young man, — or is it a road agint you expects to see, that you 'olds hup your 'ands, hand crosses 'em like to that,' sez he. ' 'Old 'ard,' sez he, ' on the short curves, or you 'll bust your precious crust,' sez he. And hasks for you, sir. This way, sir."

They entered the lodge. Islington hurried down the long Gothic hall, and opened the library door.

In an arm-chair, in the centre of the room, a man sat apparently contemplating a large, stiff, yellow hat with an enormous brim, that was placed on the floor before him. His hands rested lightly between his knees, but one foot was drawn up at the side of his chair in a peculiar manner. In the first glance that Islington gave, the attitude in some odd, irreconcilable way suggested a brake. In another moment he dashed across the room, and, holding out both hands, cried, " Yuba Bill !"

The man rose, caught Islington by the shoulders, wheeled him round, hugged him, felt of his ribs like a good-natured ogre, shook his hands violently, laughed, and then said, somewhat ruefully, "And how ever did you know me ? "

Seeing that Yuba Bill evidently regarded himself as in some elaborate disguise, Islington laughed, and suggested that it must have been instinct.

"And you?" said Bill, holding him at arm's length, and surveying him critically, — "you! — toe think — toe think — a little cuss no higher nor a trace, a boy as I've flicked outer the road with a whip time in agin, a boy ez never hed much clothes to speak of, turned into a sport!"

Islington remembered, with a thrill of ludicrous terror, that he still wore his evening dress.

"Turned," continued Yuba Bill, severely, — "turned into a restyourant waiter, — a garsong! Eh, Alfonse, bring me a patty de foy grass and an omelette, demme!"

"Dear old chap!" said Islington, laughing, and trying to put his hand over Bill's bearded mouth, "but you — _you_ don't look exactly like yourself! You're not well, Bill." And indeed, as he turned toward the light, Bill's eyes appeared cavernous, and his hair and beard thickly streaked with gray.

"Maybe it's this yer harness," said Bill, a little anxiously. "When I hitches on this yer curb" (he indicated a massive gold watch-chain with enormous links), "and mounts this 'morning star,'" (he pointed to a very large solitaire pin which had the appearance of blistering his whole shirt-front), "it kinder weighs heavy on me, Tommy. Otherwise I'm all right, my boy, — all right." But he evaded Islington's keen eye, and turned from the light.

"You have something to tell me, Bill," said Islington, suddenly, and with almost brusque directness; "out with it."

Bill did not speak, but moved uneasily toward his hat.

"You did n't come three thousand miles, without a word of warning, to talk to me of old times," said Islington, more kindly, "glad as I would have been to see you. It is n't your way, Bill, and you know it. We shall not be disturbed here," he added, in reply to an inquiring glance that Bill directed to the door, " and I am ready to hear you."

"Firstly, then," said Bill, drawing his chair nearer Islington, "answer me one question, Tommy, fair and square, and up and down."

"Go on," said Islington, with a slight smile.

"Ef I should say to you, Tommy, — say to you to-day, right here, you must come with me, — you must leave this place for a month, a year, two years maybe, perhaps forever, — is there anything that 'ud keep you, — anything, my boy, ez you could n't leave ?"

"No," said Tommy, quietly; "I am only visiting here. I thought of leaving Greyport to-day."

"But if I should say to you, Tommy, come with me on a *pascar* to Chiny, to Japan, to South Ameriky, p'r'aps, could you go ?"

"Yes," said Islington, after a slight pause.

"Thar is n't ennything," said Bill, drawing a little closer, and lowering his voice confidentially, — "ennything in the way of a young woman—you understand, Tommy—ez would keep you? They 're mighty sweet about here; and whether a man is young or old, Tommy, there's always some woman as is brake or whip to him!"

In a certain excited bitterness that character-ized the delivery of this abstract truth, Bill did not see that the young man's face flushed slightly as he answered "No."

"Then listen. It 's seven years ago, Tommy, thet I was working one o' the Pioneer coaches over from Gold Hill. Ez I stood in front o' the stage-office, the sheriff o' the county comes to me, and he sez, 'Bill,' sez he, 'I 've got a looney chap, as I 'm in charge of, taking 'im down to the 'sylum in Stockton. He 'z quiet and peaceable, but the insides don't like to ride with him. Hev you enny objec-tion to give him a lift on the box beside you?' I sez, 'No; put him up.' When I came to go and get up on that box beside him, that man, Tommy, —that man sittin' there, quiet and peaceable, was — Johnson!

"He did n't know me, my boy," Yuba Bill con-tinued, rising and putting his hands on Tommy's shoulders, — "he did n't know me. He did n't know nothing about you, nor Angel's, nor the quicksilver lode, nor even his own name. He said his name was Skaggs, but I knowd it was Johnson. Thar was times, Tommy, you might have knocked me off that box with a feather; thar was times when if the twenty-seven passengers o' that stage hed found theirselves swimming in the American River five hundred feet below the road, I never could have explained it satisfactorily to the company,—never.

"The sheriff said," Bill continued hastily, as if to preclude any interruption from the young man, —"the sheriff said he had been brought into Murphy's Camp three years before, dripping with water, and sufferin' from perkussion of the brain, and had been cared for generally by the boys 'round. When I told the sheriff I knowed 'im, I got him to leave him in my care; and I took him to 'Frisco, Tommy, to 'Frisco, and I put him in charge o' the best doctors there, and paid his board myself. There was nothin' he didn't have ez he wanted. Don't look that way, my dear boy, for God's sake, don't!"

"O Bill," said Islington, rising and staggering to the window, "why did you keep this from me?"

"Why?" said Bill, turning on him savagely,— "why? because I warn't a fool. Thar was you, winnin' your way in college; thar was you, risin' in the world, and of some account to it; Yer was an old bummer, ez good ez dead to it,—a man ez

oughter been dead afore! a man ez never denied
it! But you allus liked him better nor me," said
Bill, bitterly.

"Forgive me, Bill," said the young man, seizing
both his hands. "I know you did it for the best;
but go on."

"Thar ain't much more to tell, nor much use to
tell it, as I can see," said Bill, moodily. "He never
could be cured, the doctors said, for he had what
they called monomania, — was always talking
about his wife and darter that somebody had stole
away years ago, and plannin' revenge on that somebody. And six months ago he was missed. I
tracked him to Carson, to Salt Lake City, to Oma-
ha, to Chicago, to New York, — and here!"

"Here!" echoed Islington.

"Here! And that's what brings me here to-day.
Whethers he's crazy or well, whethers he's huntin'
you or lookin' up that other man, you must get
away from here. You mustn't see him. You and
me, Tommy, will go away on a cruise. In three
or four years he'll be dead or missing, and then
we'll come back. Come." And he rose to his feet.

"Bill," said Islington, rising also, and taking
the hand of his friend, with the same quiet obsti-
nacy that in the old days had endeared him to
Bill, "wherever he is, here or elsewhere, sane or
crazy, I shall seek and find him. Every dollar
that I have shall be his, every dollar that I have

spent shall be returned to him. I am young yet, thank God, and can work; and if there is a way out of this miserable business, I shall find it."

"I knew," said Bill, with a surliness that ill concealed his evident admiration of the calm figure before him — "I knew the partikler style of d—n fool that you was, and expected no better. Good by, then — God Almighty! who's that?"

He was on his way to the open French window, but had started back, his face quite white and bloodless, and his eyes staring. Islington ran to the window, and looked out. A white skirt vanished around the corner of the veranda. When he returned, Bill had dropped into a chair.

"It must have been Miss Masterman, I think; but what's the matter?"

"Nothing," said Bill, faintly; "have you got any whiskey handy?"

Islington brought a decanter, and, pouring out some spirits, handed the glass to Bill. Bill drained it, and then said, "Who is Miss Masterman?"

"Mr. Masterman's daughter; that is, an adopted daughter, I believe."

"Wot name?"

"I really don't know," said Islington, pettishly, more vexed than he cared to own at this questioning.

Yuba Bill rose and walked to the window.

closed it, walked back again to the door, glanced at Islington, hesitated, and then returned to his chair.

"I didn't tell you I was married, — did I?" he said suddenly, looking up in Islington's face with an unsuccessful attempt at a reckless laugh.

"No," said Islington, more pained at the manner than the words.

"Fact," said Yuba Bill. "Three years ago it was, Tommy, — three years ago!"

He looked so hard at Islington, that, feeling he was expected to say something, he asked vaguely, "Who did you marry?"

"Thet's it!" said Yuba Bill; "I can't ezactly say; partikly, though, a she devil! generally, the wife of half a dozen other men."

Accustomed, apparently, to have his conjugal infelicities a theme of mirth among men, and seeing no trace of amusement on Islington's grave face, his dogged, reckless manner softened, and, drawing his chair closer to Islington, he went on : " It all began outer this : we was coming down Watson's grade one night pretty free, when the expressman turns to me and sez, ' There's a row inside, and you'd better pull up!' I pulls up, and out hops, first a woman, and then two or three chaps swearing and cursin', and tryin' to drag some one arter them. Then it 'pear'd, Tommy, thet it was this woman's drunken husband they was go-

ing to put out for abusin' her, and strikin' her in
the coach; and if it had n't been for me, my boy,
they 'd hev left that chap thar in the road. But I
fixes matters up by putting her alongside o' me on
the box, and we drove on. She was very white,
Tommy, — for the matter o' that, she was always
one o' these very white women, that never got red
in the face, — but she never cried a whimper.
Most wimin would have cried. It was queer, but
she never cried. I thought so at the time.

"She was very tall, with a lot o' light hair me-
andering down the back of her head, as long as a
deer-skin whip-lash, and about the color. She
hed eyes thet 'd bore you through at fifty yards,
and pooty hands and feet. And when she kinder
got out o' that stiff, narvous state she was in, and
warmed up a little, and got chipper, by G—d, sir,
she was handsome, — she was that!"

A little flushed and embarrassed at his own enthusiasm, he stopped, and then said, carelessly,

They got off at Murphy's."

"Well," said Islington.

"Well, I used to see her often arter thet, and
when she was alone she allus took the box-seat.
She kinder confided her troubles to me, how her
husband got drunk and abused her; and I did n't
see much o' him, for he was away in 'Frisco arter
thet. But it was all square, Tommy, — all square
'twixt me and her.

"I got a going there a good deal, and then one day I sez to myself, 'Bill, this won't do,' and I got changed to another route. Did you ever know Jackson Filltree, Tommy?" said Bill, breaking off suddenly.

"No."

"Might have heerd of him, p'r'aps?"

"No," said Islington, impatiently.

"Jackson Filltree ran the express from White's out to Summit, 'cross the North Fork of the Yuba. One day he sez to me, 'Bill, that 's a mighty bad ford at the North Fork.' I sez, 'I believe you, Jackson.' 'It 'll git me some day, Bill, sure,' sez he. I sez, 'Why don't you take the lower ford?' 'I don't know,' sez he, 'but I can't.' So ever after, when I met him, he sez, 'That North Fork ain't got me yet.' One day I was in Sacramento, and up comes Filltree. He sez, 'I've sold out the express business on account of the North Fork, but it 's bound to get me yet, Bill, sure'; and he laughs. Two weeks after they finds his body below the ford, whar he tried to cross, comin' down from the Summit way. Folks said it was foolishness: Tommy, I sez it was Fate! The second day arter I was changed to the Placerville route, thet woman comes outer the hotel above the stage-office. Her husband, she said, was lying sick in Placerville; that 's what she said; but it was Fate, Tommy, Fate. Three months afterward, her husband takes

an overdose of morphine for delirium tremens, and
dies. There's folks ez sez she gave it to him, but
it's Fate. A year after that I married her, — Fate,
Tommy, Fate!

"I lived with her jest three months," he went
on, after a long breath, — "three months! It ain't
much time for a happy man. I've seen a good
deal o' hard life in my day, but there was days in
that three months longer than any day in my life,
— days, Tommy, when it was a toss-up whether I
should kill her or she me. But thar, I'm done.
You are a young man, Tommy, and I ain't goin'
to tell things thet, old as I am, three years ago I
could n't have believed."

When at last, with his grim face turned toward
the window, he sat silently with his clinched
hands on his knees before him, Islington asked
where his wife was now.

"Ask me no more, my boy, — no more. I've said
my say." With a gesture as of throwing down a
pair of reins before him, he rose, and walked to
the window.

"You kin understand, Tommy, why a little trip
around the world 'ud do me good. Ef you can't
go with me, well and good. But go I must."

"Not before luncheon, I hope," said a very sweet
voice, as Blanche Masterman suddenly stood before
them. "Father would never forgive me if in his
absence I permitted one of Mr. Islington's friends

to go in this way.   You will stay, won't you ? Do!
And you will give me your arm now ; and when
Mr. Islington has done staring, he will follow us
into the dining-room and introduce you."

"I have quite fallen in love with your friend,"
said Miss Blanche, as they stood in the drawing-
room looking at the figure of Bill, strolling, with
his short pipe in his mouth, through the distant
shrubbery. "He asks very queer questions, though.
He wanted to know my mother's maiden name."

"He is an honest fellow," said Islington, gravely.

"You are very much subdued.   You don't
thank me, I dare say, for keeping you and your
friend here ; but you could n't go, you know, until
father returned."

Islington smiled, but not very gayly.

"And then I think it much better for us to part
here under these frescos, don't you ?   Good by."

She extended her long, slim hand.

"Out in the sunlight there, when my eyes
were red, you were very anxious to look at me,"
she added, in a dangerous voice.

Islington raised his sad eyes to hers.   Something glittering upon her own sweet lashes trembled and fell.

"Blanche !"

She was rosy enough now, and would have with-
drawn her hand, but Islington detained it.   She
was not quite certain but that her waist was also

in jeopardy.   Yet she could not help saying, " Are
you sure that there is n't anything in the way of
a young woman that would keep you ? "

" Blanche ! " said Islington in reproachful horror.

" If gentlemen will roar out their secrets before
an open window, with a young woman lying on a
sofa on the veranda, reading a stupid French
novel, they must not be surprised if she gives
more attention to them than her book."

" Then you know all, Blanche ? "

" I know," said Blanche, " let 's see — I know
the partiklar style of — ahem ! — fool you was,
and expected no better.   Good by."   And, gliding
like a lovely and innocent milk snake out of his
grasp, she slipped away.

To the pleasant ripple of waves, the sound of
music and light voices, the yellow midsummer
moon again rose over Greyport.   It looked upon
formless masses of rock and shrubbery, wide
spaces of lawn and beach, and a shimmering
expanse of water.   It singled out particular objects, — a white sail in shore, a crystal globe upon
the lawn, and flashed upon something held between the teeth of a crouching figure scaling the
low wall of Cliffwood Lodge.   Then, as a man
and woman passed out from under the shadows of
the foliage into the open moonlight of the garden
path, the figure leaped from the wall, and stood
erect and waiting in the shadow.

It was the figure of an old man, with rolling eyes, his trembling hand grasping a long, keen knife, — a figure more pitiable than pitiless, more pathetic than terrible. But the next moment the knife was stricken from his hand, and he struggled in the firm grasp of another figure that apparently sprang from the wall beside him.

"D—n you, Masterman!" cried the old man, hoarsely; "give me fair play, and I'll kill you yet!"

"Which my name is Yuba Bill," said Bill, quietly, "and it's time this d—n fooling was stopped."

The old man glared in Bill's face savagely. "I know you. You're one of Masterman's friends, — d—n you, — let me go till I cut his heart out, — let me go! Where is my Mary? — where is my wife? — there she is! there! — there! — there! Mary!" He would have screamed, but Bill placed his powerful hand upon his mouth, as he turned in the direction of the old man's glance. Distinct in the moonlight the figures of Islington and Blanche, arm in arm, stood out upon the garden path.

"Give me my wife!" muttered the old man hoarsely, between Bill's fingers. "Where is she?"

A sudden fury passed over Yuba Bill's face. "Where is your wife?" he echoed, pressing the old man back against the garden wall, and holding him there as in a vice. "Where is your wife?" he repeated, thrusting his grim sardonic jaw and savage eyes into the old man's frightened face. "Where is Jack Adam's wife? Where is MY wife? Where is the she-devil that drove one man mad, that sent another to hell by his own hand, that eternally broke and ruined me? Where! Where! Do you ask where? In jail in Sacramento, — in jail, do you hear? — in jail for murder, Johnson, — murder!"

The old man gasped, stiffened, and then, relaxing, suddenly slipped, a mere inanimate mass, at Yuba Bill's feet. With a sudden revulsion of feeling, Yuba Bill dropped at his side, and, lifting him tenderly in his arms, whispered, "Look up, old man, Johnson! look up, for God's sake! — it 's me, — Yuba Bill! and yonder is your daughter, and — Tommy! — don't you know — Tommy, little Tommy Islington?"

Johnson's eyes slowly opened. He whispered, "Tommy! yes, Tommy! Sit by me, Tommy. But don't sit so near the bank. Don't you see how the river is rising and beckoning to me, — hissing, and boilin' over the rocks? It 's gittin higher! — hold me, Tommy, — hold me, and don't let me go yet. We 'll live to cut his heart out, Tommy, — we 'll live — we 'll — " His head sank, and the rushing river, invisible to all eyes save his, leaped toward him out of the darkness, and bore him away, no longer to the darkness, but through it to the distant, peaceful, shining sea.

HOW SANTA CLAUS CAME TO SIMP-SON'S BAR.

IT had been raining in the valley of the Sacramento. The North Fork had overflowed its banks and Rattlesnake Creek was impassable. The few boulders that had marked the summer ford at Simpson's Crossing were obliterated by a vast sheet of water stretching to the foothills. The up stage was stopped at Grangers; the last mail had been abandoned in the *tules*, the rider swimming for his life. "An area," remarked the "Sierra Avalanche," with pensive local pride, "as large as the State of Massachusetts is now under water."

Nor was the weather any better in the foothills. The mud lay deep on the mountain road; wagons that neither physical force nor moral objurgation could move from the evil ways into which they had fallen, encumbered the track, and the way to Simpson's Bar was indicated by broken-down teams and hard swearing. And farther on, cut off and inaccessible, rained upon and bedraggled, smitten by high winds and threatened by high water, Simpson's Bar, on the eve of Christmas day, 1862, clung like a swallow's nest to the rocky entablature and splintered capitals of Table Mountain, and shook in the blast.

As night shut down on the settlement, a few lights gleamed through the mist from the windows of cabins on either side of the highway now crossed and gullied by lawless streams and swept by marauding winds. Happily most of the population were gathered at Thompson's store, clustered around a red-hot stove, at which they silently spat in some accepted sense of social communion that perhaps rendered conversation unnecessary. Indeed, most methods of diversion had long since been exhausted on Simpson's Bar; high water had suspended the regular occupations on gulch and on river, and a consequent lack of money and whiskey had taken the zest from most illegitimate recreation. Even Mr. Hamlin was fain to leave the Bar with fifty dollars in his pocket, — the only amount actually realized of the large sums won by him in the successful exercise of his arduous profession. " Ef I was asked," he remarked somewhat later, — " ef I was asked to pint out a purty little village where a retired sport as did n't care for money could exercise hisself, frequent and lively, I 'd say Simpson's Bar; but for a young man with a large family depending on his exertions, it don't pay." As Mr. Hamlin's family consisted mainly of female adults, this remark is quoted rather to show the breadth of

his humor than the exact extent of his responsibilities.

Howbeit, the unconscious objects of this satire
sat that evening in the listless apathy begotten of
idleness and lack of excitement. Even the sudden
splashing of hoofs before the door did not arouse
them. Dick Bullen alone paused in the act of
scraping out his pipe, and lifted his head, but no
other one of the group indicated any interest in,
or recognition of, the man who entered.

It was a figure familiar enough to the company,
and known in Simpson's Bar as " The Old Man."
A man of perhaps fifty years ; grizzled and scant
of hair, but still fresh and youthful of complexion.
A face full of ready, but not very powerful sympathy, with a chameleon-like aptitude for taking
on the shade and color of contiguous moods and
feelings. He had evidently just left some hilarious companions, and did not at first notice the
gravity of the group, but clapped the shoulder of
the nearest man jocularly, and threw himself into
a vacant chair.

" Jest heard the best thing out, boys ! Ye know
Smiley, over yar, — Jim Smiley, — funniest man
in the Bar ? Well, Jim was jest telling the richest
yarn about — "

" Smiley 's a —— fool," interrupted a gloomy
voice.

" A particular —— skunk," added another in
sepulchral accents.

A silence followed these positive statements. The Old Man glanced quickly around the group. Then his face slowly changed. "That's so," he said reflectively, after a pause, "certingly a sort of a skunk and suthin of a fool. In course." He was silent for a moment as in painful contemplation of the unsavoriness and folly of the unpopular Smiley. "Dismal weather, ain't it?" he added, now fully embarked on the current of prevailing sentiment. "Mighty rough papers on the boys, and no show for money this season. And to-morrow's Christmas."

There was a movement among the men at this announcement, but whether of satisfaction or disgust was not plain. "Yes," continued the Old Man in the lugubrious tone he had, within the last few moments, unconsciously adopted, — "yes, Christmas, and to-night's Christmas eve. Ye see, boys, I kinder thought — that is, I sorter had an idee, jest passin' like, you know — that may be ye'd all like to come over to my house to-night and have a sort of tear round. But I suppose, now, you would n't? Don't feel like it, may be?" he added with anxious sympathy, peering into the faces of his companions.

"Well, I don't know," responded Tom Flynn with some cheerfulness. "P'r'aps we may. But how about your wife, Old Man? What does *she* say to it?"

The Old Man hesitated. His conjugal experience had not been a happy one, and the fact was known to Simpson's Bar. His first wife, a delicate, pretty little woman, had suffered keenly and secretly from the jealous suspicions of her husband, until one day he invited the whole Bar to his house to expose her infidelity. On arriving, the party found the shy, *petite* creature quietly engaged in her household duties, and retired abashed and discomfited. But the sensitive woman did not easily recover from the shock of this extraordinary outrage. It was with difficulty she regained her equanimity sufficiently to release her lover from the closet in which he was concealed and escape with him. She left a boy of three years to comfort her bereaved husband. The Old Man's present wife had been his cook. She was large, loyal, and aggressive.

Before he could reply, Joe Dimmick suggested with great directness that it was the "Old Man's house," and that, invoking the Divine Power, if the case were his own, he would invite whom he pleased, even if in so doing he imperilled his salvation. The Powers of Evil, he further remarked, should contend against him vainly. All this delivered with a terseness and vigor lost in this necessary translation.

"In course. Certainly. Thet's it," said the Old Man with a sympathetic frown. "Thar's no

trouble about *thet*. It's my own house, built every
stick on it myself. Don't you be afeard o' her,
boys. She *may* cut up a trifle rough, — ez wimmin
do, — but she'll come round." Secretly the Old
Man trusted to the exaltation of liquor and the
power of courageous example to sustain him in
such an emergency.

As yet, Dick Bullen, the oracle and leader of
Simpson's Bar, had not spoken. He now took his
pipe from his lips. "Old Man, how's that yer
Johnny gettin' on ? Seems to me he did n't look
so peart last time I seed him on the bluff heavin'
rocks at Chinamen. Did n't seem to take much
interest in it. Thar was a gang of 'em by yar
yesterday, — drownded out up the river, — and I
kinder thought o' Johnny, and how he'd miss 'em !
May be now, we'd be in the way ef he wus sick ?"

The father, evidently touched not only by this
pathetic picture of Johnny's deprivation, but by
the considerate delicacy of the speaker, hastened
to assure him that Johnny was better and that
a "little fun might 'liven him up." Whereupon
Dick arose, shook himself, and saying, " I 'm ready.
Lead the way, Old Man: here goes," himself led
the way with a leap, a characteristic howl, and
darted out into the night. As he passed through
the outer room he caught up a blazing brand from
the hearth. The action was repeated by the rest
of the party, closely following and elbowing each

other, and before the astonished proprietor of
Thompson's grocery was aware of the intention of
his guests, the room was deserted.

The night was pitchy dark. In the first gust of
wind their temporary torches were extinguished,
and only the red brands dancing and flitting in
the gloom like drunken will-o'-the-wisps indicated
their whereabouts.   Their way led up Pine-Tree
Cañon, at the head of which a broad, low, bark-
thatched cabin burrowed in the mountain-side.   It
was the home of the Old Man, and the entrance to
the tunnel in which he worked when he worked at
all.   Here the crowd paused for a moment, out of
delicate deference to their host, who came up panting in the rear.

" P'r'aps ye 'd better hold on a second out yer,
whilst I go in and see thet things is all right,"
said the Old Man, with an indifference he was far
from feeling.   The suggestion was graciously accepted, the door opened and closed on the host,
and the crowd, leaning their backs against the wall
and cowering under the eaves, waited and listened.

For a few moments there was no sound but the
dripping of water from the eaves, and the stir and
rustle of wrestling boughs above them.   Then the
men became uneasy, and whispered suggestion
and suspicion passed from the one to the other.
" Reckon she 's caved in his head the first lick ! "
" Decoyed him inter the tunnel and barred him

up, likely." " Got him down and sittin' on him."
" Prob'ly bilin suthin to heave on us : stand clear
the door, boys ! " For just then the latch clicked,
the door slowly opened, and a voice said, " Come
in out o' the wet."

The voice was neither that of the Old Man nor
of his wife. It was the voice of a small boy, its
weak treble broken by that preternatural hoarse-
ness which only vagabondage and the habit of pre-
mature self-assertion can give. It was the face of
a small boy that looked up at theirs, — a face that
might have been pretty and even refined but that
it was darkened by evil knowledge from within,
and dirt and hard experience from without. He
had a blanket around his shoulders and had evidently just risen from his bed. " Come in," he repeated, " and don't make no noise. The Old Man 's
in there talking to mar," he continued, pointing to
an adjacent room which seemed to be a kitchen,
from which the Old Man's voice came in deprecat-
ing accents. " Let me be," he added, querulously,
to Dick Bullen, who had caught him up, blanket
and all, and was affecting to toss him into the fire,
" let go o' me, you d—d old fool, d' ye hear ? "

Thus adjured, Dick Bullen lowered Johnny to
the ground with a smothered laugh, while the
men, entering quietly, ranged themselves around a
long table of rough boards which occupied the
centre of the room. Johnny then gravely pro-

ceeded to a cupboard and brought out several articles which he deposited on the table. "Thar's whiskey. And crackers. And red herons. And cheese." He took a bite of the latter on his way to the table. "And sugar." He scooped up a mouthful *en route* with a small and very dirty hand. "And terbacker. Thar's dried appils too on the shelf, but I don't admire 'em. Appils is swellin'. Thar," he concluded, "now wade in, and don't be afeard. *I* don't mind the old woman. She don't b'long to *me*. S'long."

He had stepped to the threshold of a small room, scarcely larger than a closet, partitioned off from the main apartment, and holding in its dim recess a small bed. He stood there a moment looking at the company, his bare feet peeping from the blanket, and nodded.

"Hello, Johnny! You ain't goin' to turn in agin, are ye?" said Dick.

"Yes, I are." responded Johnny, decidedly.

"Why, wot's up, old fellow?"

"I'm sick."

"How sick?"

"I've got a fevier. And childblains. And roomatiz," returned Johnny, and vanished within. After a moment's pause, he added in the dark, apparently from under the bedclothes, — "And biles!"

There was an embarrassing silence. The men

looked at each other, and at the fire. Even with the appetizing banquet before them, it seemed as if they might again fall into the despondency of Thompson's grocery, when the voice of the Old Man, incautiously lifted, came deprecatingly from the kitchen.

"Certainly! Thet's so. In course they is. A gang o' lazy drunken loafers, and that ar Dick Bullen's the ornariest of all. Did n't hev no more *sabe* than to come round yar with sickness in the house and no provision. Thet's what I said: 'Bullen,' sez I, 'it's crazy drunk you are, or a fool,' sez I, 'to think o' such a thing.' 'Staples,' I sez, 'be you a man, Staples, and 'spect to raise h—ll under my roof and invalids lyin' round?' But they would come,— they would. Thet's wot you must 'spect o' such trash as lays round the Bar."

A burst of laughter from the men followed this unfortunate exposure. Whether it was overheard in the kitchen, or whether the Old Man's irate companion had just then exhausted all other modes of expressing her contemptuous indignation, I cannot say, but a back door was suddenly slammed with great violence. A moment later and the Old Man reappeared, haply unconscious of the cause of the late hilarious outburst, and smiled blandly.

"The old woman thought she'd jest run over to Mrs. McFadden's for a sociable call," he explained, with jaunty indifference, as he took a seat at the board.

Oddly enough it needed this untoward incident to relieve the embarrassment that was beginning to be felt by the party, and their natural audacity returned with their host. I do not propose to record the convivialities of that evening. The inquisitive reader will accept the statement that the conversation was characterized by the same intellectual exaltation, the same cautious reverence, the same fastidious delicacy, the same rhetorical precision, and the same logical and coherent discourse somewhat later in the evening, which distinguish similar gatherings of the masculine sex in more civilized localities and under more favorable auspices. No glasses were broken in the absence of any; no liquor was uselessly spilt on floor or table in the scarcity of that article.

It was nearly midnight when the festivities were interrupted. "Hush," said Dick Bullen, holding up his hand. It was the querulous voice of Johnny from his adjacent closet: "O dad!"

The Old Man arose hurriedly and disappeared in the closet. Presently he reappeared. "His rheumatiz is coming on agin bad," he explained, "and he wants rubbin'." He lifted the demijohn of whiskey from the table and shook it. It was empty. Dick Bullen put down his tin cup with an embarrassed laugh. So did the others. The

Old Man examined their contents and said hope-
fully, "I reckon that's enough; he don't need much.
You hold on all o' you for a spell, and I'll be
back"; and vanished in the closet with an old
flannel shirt and the whiskey. The door closed
but imperfectly, and the following dialogue was
distinctly audible: —

"Now, sonny, whar does she ache worst?"

"Sometimes over yar and sometimes under yer;
but it's most powerful from yer to yer. Rub yer,
dad."

A silence seemed to indicate a brisk rubbing.
Then Johnny:

"Hevin' a good time out yer, dad?"

"Yes, sonny."

"To-morrer's Chrismiss, — ain't it?"

"Yes, sonny. How does she feel now?"

"Better. Rub a little furder down. Wot's
Chrismiss, anyway? Wot's it all about?"

"O, it's a day."

This exhaustive definition was apparently satisfactory, for there was a silent interval of rubbing.
Presently Johnny again:

"Mar sez that everywhere else but yer everybody gives things to everybody Chrismiss, and
then she jist waded inter you. She sez thar's a
man they call Sandy Claws, not a white man, you
know, but a kind o' Chinemin, comes down the
chimbley night afore Chrismiss and gives things

to chillern, — boys like me.   Puts 'em in their
butes ! Thet's what she tried to play upon me.
Easy now, pop, whar are you rubbin' to, — thet's
a mile from the place. She jest made that up,
did n't she, jest to aggrewate me and you ? Don't
rub thar. . . . . Why, dad !"

In the great quiet that seemed to have fallen
upon the house the sigh of the near pines and the
drip of leaves without was very distinct. Johnny's voice, too, was lowered as he went on, " Don't
you take on now, fur I 'm gettin' all right fast.
Wot 's the boys doin' out thar ? "

The Old Man partly opened the door and peered
through. His guests were sitting there sociably
enough, and there were a few silver coins and a
lean buckskin purse on the table.   " Bettin' on
suthin, — some little game or 'nother. They 're
all right," he replied to Johnny, and recommenced
his rubbing.

" I 'd like to take a hand and win some money,"
said Johnny, reflectively, after a pause.

The Old Man glibly repeated what was evidently
a familiar formula, that if Johnny would wait until
he struck it rich in the tunnel he 'd have lots of
money, etc., etc.

"Yes," said Johnny, "but you don't. And
whether you strike it or I win it, it 's about the
same. It 's all luck. But it 's mighty cur'o's
about Chrismiss, — ain't it ? Why do they call
it Chrismiss ? "

Perhaps from some instinctive deference to the overhearing of his guests, or from some vague sense of incongruity, the Old Man's reply was so low as to be inaudible beyond the room.

" Yes," said Johnny, with some slight abatement of interest, " I 've heerd o' *him* before.   Thar, that 'll do, dad.   I don't ache near so bad as I did. Now wrap me tight in this yer blanket.   So. Now," he added in a muffled whisper, " sit down yer by me till I go asleep."   To assure himself of obedience, he disengaged one hand from the blanket and, grasping his father's sleeve, again composed himself to rest.

For some moments the Old Man waited patiently.   Then the unwonted stillness of the house excited his curiosity, and without moving from the bed, he cautiously opened the door with his disengaged hand, and looked into the main room. To his infinite surprise it was dark and deserted. But even then a smouldering log on the hearth broke, and by the upspringing blaze he saw the figure of Dick Bullen sitting by the dying embers.

" Hello ! "

Dick started, rose, and came somewhat unsteadily toward him.

" Whar 's the boys ? " said the Old Man.

" Gone up the cañon on a little *pasear*.   They 're coming back for me in a minit.   I 'm waitin' round for 'em.   What are you starin' at, Old Man ? "

he added with a forced laugh ; " do you think I 'm drunk ? "

The Old Man might have been pardoned the supposition, for Dick's eyes were humid and his face flushed.   He loitered and lounged back to the chimney, yawned, shook himself, buttoned up his coat and laughed.   " Liquor ain't so plenty as that, Old Man.   Now don't you git up," he continued, as the Old Man made a movement to release his sleeve from Johnny's hand.   " Don't you mind manners.   Sit jest whar you be ; I 'm goin' in a jiffy.   Thar, that 's them now."

There was a low tap at the door.   Dick Bullen opened it quickly, nodded " Good night " to his host, and disappeared.   The Old Man would have followed him but for the hand that still unconsciously grasped his sleeve.   He could have easily disengaged it : it was small, weak, and emaciated. But perhaps because it *was* small, weak, and emaciated, he changed his mind, and, drawing his chair closer to the bed, rested his head upon it.   In this defenceless attitude the potency of his earlier potations surprised him.   The room flickered and faded before his eyes, reappeared, faded again, went out, and left him — asleep.

Meantime Dick Bullen, closing the door, confronted his companions.   " Are you ready ? " said Staples.   " Ready," said Dick ; " what 's the time ? " " Past twelve," was the reply ; " can you make it ?

— it's nigh on fifty miles, the round trip hither and yon." "I reckon," returned Dick, shortly. "Whar's the mare?" "Bill and Jack's holdin' her at the crossin'." "Let 'em hold on a minit longer," said Dick.

He turned and re-entered the house softly. By the light of the guttering candle and dying fire he saw that the door of the little room was open. He stepped toward it on tiptoe and looked in. The Old Man had fallen back in his chair, snoring, his helpless feet thrust out in a line with his collapsed shoulders, and his hat pulled over his eyes. Beside him, on a narrow wooden bedstead, lay Johnny, muffled tightly in a blanket that hid all save a strip of forehead and a few curls damp with perspiration. Dick Bullen made a step forward, hesitated, and glanced over his shoulder into the deserted room. Everything was quiet. With a sudden resolution he parted his huge mustaches with both hands and stooped over the sleeping boy. But even as he did so a mischievous blast, lying in wait, swooped down the chimney, rekindled the hearth, and lit up the room with a shameless glow from which Dick fled in bashful terror.

His companions were already waiting for him at the crossing. Two of them were struggling in the darkness with some strange misshapen bulk, which as Dick came nearer took the semblance of a great yellow horse.

It was the mare. She was not a pretty picture.
From her Roman nose to her rising haunches,
from her arched spine hidden by the stiff *machillas*
of a Mexican saddle, to her thick, straight, bony
legs, there was not a line of equine grace. In her
half-blind but wholly vicious white eyes, in her
protruding under lip, in her monstrous color, there
was nothing but ugliness and vice.

"Now then," said Staples, "stand cl'ar of her
heels, boys, and up with you. Don't miss your
first holt of her mane, and mind ye get your off
stirrup *quick*. Ready!"

There was a leap, a scrambling struggle, a
bound, a wild retreat of the crowd, a circle of
flying hoofs, two springless leaps that jarred the
earth, a rapid play and jingle of spurs, a plunge,
and then the voice of Dick somewhere in the
darkness, "All right!"

"Don't take the lower road back onless you 're
hard pushed for time! Don't hold her in down
hill! We 'll be at the ford at five. G' lang!
Hoopa! Mula! GO!"

A splash, a spark struck from the ledge in the
road, a clatter in the rocky cut beyond, and Dick
was gone.

    .   .   .   .   .

Sing, O Muse, the ride of Richard Bullen! Sing,
O Muse of chivalrous men! the sacred quest, the
doughty deeds, the battery of low churls, the fear-

some ride and grewsome perils of the Flower of
Simpson's Bar! Alack! she is dainty, this Muse!
She will have none of this bucking brute and
swaggering, ragged rider, and I must fain follow
him in prose, afoot!

It was one o'clock, and yet he had only gained
Rattlesnake Hill. For in that time Jovita had re-
hearsed to him all her imperfections and practised
all her vices. Thrice had she stumbled. Twice
had she thrown up her Roman nose in a straight
line with the reins, and, resisting bit and spur,
struck out madly across country. Twice had she
reared, and, rearing, fallen backward; and twice
had the agile Dick, unharmed, regained his seat
before she found her vicious legs again. And a
mile beyond them, at the foot of a long hill, was
Rattlesnake Creek. Dick knew that here was the
crucial test of his ability to perform his enterprise,
set his teeth grimly, put his knees well into her
flanks, and changed his defensive tactics to brisk
aggression. Bullied and maddened, Jovita began
the descent of the hill. Here the artful Richard
pretended to hold her in with ostentatious objurgation and well-feigned cries of alarm. It is unnecessary to add that Jovita instantly ran away.
Nor need I state the time made in the descent; it
is written in the chronicles of Simpson's Bar.
Enough that in another moment, as it seemed to
Dick, she was splashing on the overflowed banks

of Rattlesnake Creek. As Dick expected, the momentum she had acquired carried her beyond the point of balking, and, holding her well together for a mighty leap, they dashed into the middle of the swiftly flowing current. A few moments of kicking, wading, and swimming, and Dick drew a long breath on the opposite bank.

The road from Rattlesnake Creek to Red Mountain was tolerably level. Either the plunge in Rattlesnake Creek had dampened her baleful fire, or the art which led to it had shown her the superior wickedness of her rider, for Jovita no longer wasted her surplus energy in wanton conceits. Once she bucked, but it was from force of habit; once she shied, but it was from a new freshly painted meeting-house at the crossing of the county road. Hollows, ditches, gravelly deposits, patches of freshly springing grasses, flew from beneath her rattling hoofs. She began to smell unpleasantly, once or twice she coughed slightly, but there was no abatement of her strength or speed. By two o'clock he had passed Red Mountain and begun the descent to the plain. Ten minutes later the driver of the fast Pioneer coach was overtaken and passed by a " man on a Pinto hoss," — an event sufficiently notable for remark. At half past two Dick rose in his stirrups with a great shout. Stars were glittering through the rifted clouds, and beyond him, out of the plain, rose two spires, a

flagstaff, and a straggling line of black objects.
Dick jingled his spurs and swung his *riata*, Jovita
bounded forward, and in another moment they
swept into Tuttleville and drew up before the
wooden piazza of "The Hotel of All Nations."

What transpired that night at Tuttleville is not
strictly a part of this record.   Briefly I may state,
however, that after Jovita had been handed over
to a sleepy ostler, whom she at once kicked into
unpleasant consciousness, Dick sallied out with
the bar-keeper for a tour of the sleeping town.
Lights still gleamed from a few saloons and gam-
bling-houses; but, avoiding these, they stopped
before several closed shops, and by persistent tap-
ping and judicious outcry roused the proprietors
from their beds, and made them unbar the doors
of their magazines and expose their wares.   Sometimes they were met by curses, but oftener by interest and some concern in their needs, and the
interview was invariably concluded by a drink.
It was three o'clock before this pleasantry was
given over, and with a small waterproof bag of
india-rubber strapped on his shoulders Dick returned to the hotel.   But here he was waylaid by
Beauty, — Beauty opulent in charms, affluent in
dress, persuasive in speech, and Spanish in accent!
In vain she repeated the invitation in "Excelsior,"
happily scorned by all Alpine-climbing youth, and
rejected by this child of the Sierras, — a rejection

softened in this instance by a laugh and his last
gold coin. And then he sprang to the saddle and
dashed down the lonely street and out into the
lonelier plain, where presently the lights, the black
line of houses, the spires, and the flagstaff sank
into the earth behind him again and were lost in
the distance.

The storm had cleared away, the air was brisk
and cold, the outlines of adjacent landmarks were
distinct, but it was half past four before Dick
reached the meeting-house and the crossing of the
county road. To avoid the rising grade he had
taken a longer and more circuitous road, in whose
viscid mud Jovita sank fetlock deep at every
bound. It was a poor preparation for a steady
ascent of five miles more; but Jovita, gathering
her legs under her, took it with her usual blind,
unreasoning fury, and a half-hour later reached
the long level that led to Rattlesnake Creek. Another half-hour would bring him to the creek. He
threw the reins lightly upon the neck of the mare,
chirruped to her, and began to sing.

Suddenly Jovita shied with a bound that would
have unseated a less practised rider. Hanging to
her rein was a figure that had leaped from the
bank, and at the same time from the road before
her arose a shadowy horse and rider. "Throw up
your hands," commanded this second apparition,
with an oath.

Dick felt the mare tremble, quiver, and apparently sink under him.   He knew what it meant and was prepared.

"Stand aside, Jack Simpson, I know you, you d—d thief.   Let me pass or — "

He did not finish the sentence.   Jovita rose straight in the air with a terrific bound, throwing the figure from her bit with a single shake of her vicious head, and charged with deadly malevolence down on the impediment before her.   An oath, a pistol-shot, horse and highwayman rolled over in the road, and the next moment Jovita was a hundred yards away.   But the good right arm of her rider, shattered by a bullet, dropped helplessly at his side.

Without slacking his speed he shifted the reins to his left hand.   But a few moments later he was obliged to halt and tighten the saddle-girths that had slipped in the onset.   This in his crippled condition took some time.   He had no fear of pursuit, but looking up he saw that the eastern stars were already paling, and that the distant peaks had lost their ghostly whiteness, and now stood out blackly against a lighter sky.   Day was upon him.   Then completely absorbed in a single idea, he forgot the pain of his wound, and mounting again dashed on toward Rattlesnake Creek. But now Jovita's breath came broken by gasps, Dick reeled in his saddle, and brighter and brighter grew the sky.

Ride, Richard; run, Jovita; linger, O day!

For the last few rods there was a roaring in his ears. Was it exhaustion from loss of blood, or what? He was dazed and giddy as he swept down the hill, and did not recognize his surroundings. Had he taken the wrong road, or was this Rattlesnake Creek?

It was. But the brawling creek he had swam a few hours before had risen, more than doubled its volume, and now rolled a swift and resistless river between him and Rattlesnake Hill. For the first time that night Richard's heart sank within him. The river, the mountain, the quickening east, swam before his eyes. He shut them to recover his self-control. In that brief interval, by some fantastic mental process, the little room at Simpson's Bar and the figures of the sleeping father and son rose upon him. He opened his eyes wildly, cast off his coat, pistol, boots, and saddle, bound his precious pack tightly to his shoulders, grasped the bare flanks of Jovita with his bared knees, and with a shout dashed into the yellow water. A cry rose from the opposite bank as the head of a man and horse struggled for a few moments against the battling current, and then were swept away amidst uprooted trees and whirling drift-wood.

    .   .   .   .   .

The Old Man started and woke. The fire on

the hearth was dead, the candle in the outer room flickering in its socket, and somebody was rapping at the door. He opened it, but fell back with a cry before the dripping, half-naked figure that reeled against the doorpost.

"Dick?"

"Hush! Is he awake yet?"

"No, — but, Dick? —"

"Dry up, you old fool! Get me some whiskey *quick!*" The Old Man flew and returned with — an empty bottle! Dick would have sworn, but his strength was not equal to the occasion. He staggered, caught at the handle of the door, and motioned to the Old Man.

"Thar's suthin' in my pack yer for Johnny. Take it off. I can't."

The Old Man unstrapped the pack and laid it before the exhausted man.

"Open it, quick!"

He did so with trembling fingers. It contained only a few poor toys, — cheap and barbaric enough, goodness knows, but bright with paint and tinsel. One of them was broken; another, I fear, was irretrievably ruined by water; and on the third — ah me! there was a cruel spot.

"It don't look like much, that's a fact," said Dick, ruefully. . . . . "But it's the best we could do. . . . . Take 'em, Old Man, and put 'em in his stocking, and tell him — tell him, you know —

hold me, Old Man — " The Old Man caught at his sinking figure. " Tell him," said Dick, with a weak little laugh, — " tell him Sandy Claus has come."

And even so, bedraggled, ragged, unshaven, and unshorn, with one arm hanging helplessly at his side, Santa Claus came to Simpson's Bar and fell fainting on the first threshold. The Christmas dawn came slowly after, touching the remoter peaks with the rosy warmth of ineffable love. And it looked so tenderly on Simpson's Bar that the whole mountain, as if caught in a generous action, blushed to the skies.

THE PRINCESS BOB AND HER FRIENDS.

S HE was a Klamath Indian. Her title was, I
think, a compromise between her claim as
daughter of a chief, and gratitude to her earliest
white protector, whose name, after the Indian fashion, she had adopted. "Bob" Walker had taken
her from the breast of her dead mother at a time
when the sincere volunteer soldiery of the California frontier were impressed with the belief that
extermination was the manifest destiny of the Indian race. He had with difficulty restrained the
noble zeal of his compatriots long enough to con-
vince them that the exemption of one Indian baby
would not invalidate this theory. And he took
her to his home, — a pastoral clearing on the banks
of the Salmon River, — where she was cared for
after a frontier fashion.

Before she was nine years old, she had exhausted
the scant kindliness of the thin, overworked Mrs.
Walker. As a playfellow of the young Walkers
she was unreliable; as a nurse for the baby she
was inefficient. She lost the former in the track-
less depths of a redwood forest; she basely abandoned the latter in an extemporized cradle, hang-

ing like a chrysalis to a convenient bough. She
lied and she stole, — two unpardonable sins in a
frontier community, where truth was a necessity
and provisions were the only property.   Worse
than this, the outskirts of the clearing were sometimes haunted by blanketed tatterdemalions with
whom she had mysterious confidences.   Mr.
Walker more than once regretted his indiscreet
humanity; but she presently relieved him of responsibility, and possibly of bloodguiltiness, by
disappearing entirely.

When she reappeared, it was at the adjacent
village of Logport, in the capacity of housemaid to
a trader's wife, who, joining some little culture to
considerable conscientiousness, attempted to in-
struct her charge.   But the Princess proved an un-
satisfactory pupil to even so liberal a teacher.   She
accepted the alphabet with great good-humor, but
always as a pleasing and recurring novelty, in
which all interest expired at the completion of
each lesson.   She found a thousand uses for her
books and writing materials other than those
known to civilized children.   She made a curious
necklace of bits of slate-pencil, she constructed a
miniature canoe from the pasteboard covers of her
primer, she bent her pens into fish-hooks, and tattooed the faces of her younger companions with
blue ink.   Religious instruction she received as
good-humoredly, and learned to pronounce the

name of the Deity with a cheerful familiarity that
shocked her preceptress.   Nor could her reverence
be reached through analogy; she knew nothing of
the Great Spirit, and professed entire ignorance of
the Happy Hunting-Grounds.   Yet she attended
divine service regularly, and as regularly asked
for a hymn-book; and it was only through the
discovery that she had collected twenty-five of
these volumes and had hidden them behind the
woodpile, that her connection with the First Baptist Church of Logport ceased.   She would occasionally abandon these civilized and Christian
privileges, and disappear from her home, returning
after several days of absence with an odor of bark
and fish, and a peace-offering to her mistress in
the shape of venison or game.

To add to her troubles, she was now fourteen,
and, according to the laws of her race, a woman.
I do not think the most romantic fancy would
have called her pretty.   Her complexion defied
most of those ambiguous similes through which
poets unconsciously apologize for any deviation
from the Caucasian standard.   It was not wine
nor amber colored; if anything, it was smoky.
Her face was tattooed with red and white lines on
one cheek, as if a fine-toothed comb had been
drawn from cheek-bone to jaw, and, but for the
good-humor that beamed from her small berry-like
eyes and shone in her white teeth, would have

been repulsive. She was short and stout. In her scant drapery and unrestrained freedom she was hardly statuesque, and her more unstudied attitudes were marred by a simian habit of softly scratching her left ankle with the toes of her right foot, in moments of contemplation.

I think I have already shown enough to indicate the incongruity of her existence with even the low standard of civilization that obtained at Logport in the year 1860. It needed but one more fact to prove the far-sighted political sagacity and prophetic ethics of those sincere advocates of extermination, to whose virtues I have done but scant justice in the beginning of this article. This fact was presently furnished by the Princess. After one of her periodical disappearances, — this time unusually prolonged, — she astonished Logport by returning with a half-breed baby of a week old in her arms. That night a meeting of the hard-featured serious matrons of Logport was held at Mrs. Brown's. The immediate banishment of the Princess was demanded. Soft-hearted Mrs. Brown endeavored vainly to get a mitigation or suspension of the sentence. But, as on a former occasion, the Princess took matters into her own hands. A few mornings afterwards, a wicker cradle containing an Indian baby was found hanging on the handle of the door of the First Baptist Church. It was the Parthian arrow of the flying

Princess. From that day Logport knew her no more.

It had been a bright clear day on the upland, so clear that the ramparts of Fort Jackson and the flagstaff were plainly visible twelve miles away from the long curving peninsula that stretched a bared white arm around the peaceful waters of Logport Bay. It had been a clear day upon the sea-shore, albeit the air was filled with the flying spume and shifting sand of a straggling beach whose low dunes were dragged down by the long surges of the Pacific and thrown up again by the tumultuous trade-winds. But the sun had gone down in a bank of fleecy fog that was beginning to roll in upon the beach. Gradually the headland at the entrance of the harbor and the light-house disappeared, then the willow fringe that marked the line of Salmon River vanished, and the ocean was gone. A few sails still gleamed on the waters of the bay; but the advancing fog wiped them out one by one, crept across the steel-blue expanse, swallowed up the white mills and single spire of Logport, and, joining with reinforce-ments from the marshes, moved solemnly upon the hills. Ten minutes more and the landscape was utterly blotted out; simultaneously the wind died away, and a death-like silence stole over sea and shore. The faint clang, high overhead, of un-

seen brent, the nearer call of invisible plover, the
lap and wash of undistinguishable waters, and the
monotonous roll of the vanished ocean, were the
only sounds.   As night deepened, the far-off
booming of the fog-bell on the headland at intervals stirred the thick air.

Hard by the shore of the bay, and half hidden
by a drifting sand-hill, stood a low nondescript
structure, to whose composition sea and shore had
equally contributed. It was built partly of logs
and partly of driftwood and tarred canvas. Joined
to one end of the main building — the ordinary
log-cabin of the settler — was the half-round pilot-
house of some wrecked steamer, while the other
gable terminated in half of a broken whale-boat.
Nailed against the boat were the dried skins of
wild animals, and scattered about lay the flotsam
and jetsam of many years' gathering, — bamboo
crates, casks, hatches, blocks, oars, boxes, part of a
whale's vertebræ, and the blades of sword-fish.
Drawn up on the beach of a little cove before the
house lay a canoe. As the night thickened and
the fog grew more dense, these details grew imper-
ceptible, and only the windows of the pilot-house,
lit up by a roaring fire within the hut, gleamed
redly through the mist.

By this fire, beneath a ship's lamp that swung
from the roof, two figures were seated, a man and
a woman. The man, broad-shouldered and heav-

ily bearded, stretched his listless powerful length beyond a broken bamboo chair, with his eyes fixed on the fire. The woman crouched cross-legged upon the broad earthen hearth, with her eyes blinkingly fixed on her companion. They were small, black, round, berry-like eyes, and as the firelight shone upon her smoky face, with its one striped cheek of gorgeous brilliancy, it was plainly the Princess Bob and no other.

Not a word was spoken. They had been sitting thus for more than an hour, and there was about their attitude a suggestion that silence was habitual. Once or twice the man rose and walked up and down the narrow room, or gazed absently from the windows of the pilot-house, but never by look or sign betrayed the slightest consciousness of his companion. At such times the Princess from her nest by the fire followed him with eyes of canine expectancy and wistfulness. But he would as inevitably return to his contemplation of the fire, and the Princess to her blinking watchfulness of his face.

They had sat there silent and undisturbed for many an evening in fair weather and foul. They had spent many a day in sunshine and storm, gathering the unclaimed spoil of sea and shore. They had kept these mute relations, varied only by the incidents of the hunt or meagre household duties, for three years, ever since the man, wandering moodily over the lonely sands, had fallen upon the half-starved woman lying in the little hollow where she had crawled to die. It had seemed as if they would never be disturbed, until now, when the Princess started, and, with the instinct of her race, bent her ear to the ground.

The wind had risen and was rattling the tarred canvas. But in another moment there plainly came from without the hut the sound of voices. Then followed a rap at the door; then another rap; and then, before they could rise to their feet, the door was flung briskly open.

" I beg your pardon," said a pleasant but somewhat decided contralto voice, " but I don't think you heard me knock. Ah, I see you did not. May I come in ? "

There was no reply. Had the battered figurehead of the Goddess of Liberty, which lay deeply embedded in the sand on the beach, suddenly appeared at the door demanding admittance, the occupants of the cabin could not have been more speechlessly and hopelessly astonished than at the form which stood in the open doorway.

It was that of a slim, shapely, elegantly dressed young woman. A scarlet-lined silken hood was half thrown back from the shining mass of the black hair that covered her small head; from her pretty shoulders dropped a fur cloak, only re-

strained by a cord and tassel in her small gloved
hand. Around her full throat was a double necklace of large white beads, that by some cunning
feminine trick relieved with its infantile suggestion the strong decision of her lower face.

"Did you say yes? Ah, thank you. We may
come in, Barker." (Here a shadow in a blue
army overcoat followed her into the cabin, touched
its cap respectfully, and then stood silent and
erect against the wall.) "Don't disturb yourself
in the least, I beg. What a distressingly unpleasant night! Is this your usual climate?"

Half graciously, half absently overlooking the
still embarrassed silence of the group, she went
on: "We started from the fort over three hours
ago, — three hours ago, was n't it, Barker?" (the
erect Barker touched his cap,) — "to go to Captain Emmons's quarters on Indian Island, — I
think you call it Indian Island, don't you?" (she
was appealing to the awe-stricken Princess,) —
"and we got into the fog and lost our way; that
is, Barker lost his way," (Barker touched his cap
deprecatingly,) "and goodness knows where we
did n't wander to until we mistook your light for
the lighthouse and pulled up here. No, no, pray
keep your seat, do! Really I must insist."

Nothing could exceed the languid grace of the
latter part of this speech, — nothing except the
easy unconsciousness with which she glided by

the offered chair of her stammering, embarrassed host and stood beside the open hearth.

"Barker will tell you," she continued, warming her feet by the fire, "that I am Miss Portfire, daughter of Major Portfire, commanding the post. Ah, excuse me, child !" (She had accidentally trodden upon the bare yellow toes of the Princess.) "Really, I did not know you were there. I am very near-sighted." (In confirmation of her statement, she put to her eyes a dainty double eye-glass that dangled from her neck.) "It's a shocking thing to be near-sighted, is n't it ?"

If the shamefaced uneasy man to whom this remark was addressed could have found words to utter the thought that even in his confusion struggled uppermost in his mind, he would, looking at the bold, dark eyes that questioned him, have denied the fact. But he only stammered, "Yes." The next moment, however, Miss Portfire had apparently forgotten him and was examining the Princess through her glass.

"And what is your name, child ?"

The Princess, beatified by the eyes and eye-glass, showed all her white teeth at once, and softly scratched her leg.

"Bob."

"Bob ? What a singular name !"

Miss Portfire's host here hastened to explain the origin of the Princess's title.

"Then *you* are Bob."   (Eye-glass.)

"No, my name is Grey, — John Grey." And he actually achieved a bow where awkwardness was rather the air of imperfectly recalling a forgotten habit.

"Grey ? — ah, let me see.   Yes, certainly.   You are Mr. Grey the recluse, the hermit, the philosopher, and all that sort of thing.   Why, certainly ; Dr. Jones, our surgeon, has told me all about you. Dear me, how interesting a rencontre !   Lived all alone here for seven — was it seven years ? — yes, I remember now.   Existed quite *au naturel*, one might say.   How odd !   Not that I know anything about that sort of thing, you know.   I 've lived always among people, and am really quite a stranger, I assure you.   But honestly, Mr. — I beg your pardon — Mr. Grey, how do you like it ? "

She had quietly taken his chair and thrown her cloak and hood over its back, and was now thoughtfully removing her gloves.   Whatever were the arguments, — and they were doubtless many and profound, — whatever the experience, — and it was doubtless hard and satisfying enough, — by which this unfortunate man had justified his life for the last seven years, somehow they suddenly became trivial and terribly ridiculous before this simple but practical question.

"Well, you shall tell me all about it after you

have given me something to eat. We will have
time enough; Barker cannot find his way back
in this fog to-night. Now don't put yourselves
to any trouble on my account. Barker will assist."

Barker came forward. Glad to escape the scrutiny of his guest, the hermit gave a few rapid
directions to the Princess in her native tongue,
and disappeared in the shed. Left a moment
alone, Miss Portfire took a quick, half-audible,
feminine inventory of the cabin. "Books, guns,
skins, *one* chair, *one* bed, no pictures, and no look-
ing-glass!" She took a book from the swinging
shelf and resumed her seat by the fire as the Princess re-entered with fresh fuel. But while kneel-
ing on the hearth the Princess chanced to look up
and met Miss Portfire's dark eyes over the edge
of her book.

"Bob!"

The Princess showed her teeth.

"Listen. Would you like to have fine clothes,
rings, and beads like these, to have your hair nicely
combed and put up so? Would you?"

The Princess nodded violently.

"Would you like to live with me and have
them? Answer quickly. Don't look round for
him. Speak for yourself. Would you? Hush;
never mind now."

The hermit re-entered, and the Princess, blinking, retreated into the shadow of the whale-boat shed, from which she did not emerge even when the homely repast of cold venison, ship biscuit, and tea was served. Miss Portfire noticed her absence: "You really must not let me interfere with your usual simple ways. Do you know this is exceedingly interesting to me, so pastoral and patriarchal and all that sort of thing. I must insist upon the Princess coming back; really, I must."

But the Princess was not to be found in the shed, and Miss Portfire, who the next minute seemed to have forgotten all about her, took her place in the single chair before an extemporized table. Barker stood behind her, and the hermit leaned against the fireplace. Miss Portfire's appetite did not come up to her protestations. For the first time in seven years it occurred to the hermit that his ordinary victual might be improved. He stammered out something to that effect.

"I have eaten better, and worse," said Miss Portfire, quietly.

"But I thought you — that is, you said —"

"I spent a year in the hospitals, when father was on the Potomac," returned Miss Portfire, composedly. After a pause she continued: "You remember after the second Bull Run — But, dear me! I beg your pardon; of course, you know nothing about the war and all that sort of thing, and don't care." (She put up her eye-glass and quietly surveyed his broad muscular figure against the chimney.) "Or, perhaps, your prejudices — But then, as a hermit you know you have no politics, of course. Please don't let me bore you."

To have been strictly consistent, the hermit should have exhibited no interest in this topic. Perhaps it was owing to some quality in the narrator, but he was constrained to beg her to continue in such phrases as his unfamiliar lips could command. So that, little by little, Miss Portfire yielded up incident and personal observation of the contest then raging; with the same half-abstracted, half-unconcerned air that seemed habitual to her, she told the stories of privation, of suffering, of endurance, and of sacrifice. With the same assumption of timid deference that concealed her great self-control, she talked of principles and rights. Apparently without enthusiasm and without effort, of which his morbid nature would have been suspicious, she sang the great American Iliad in a way that stirred the depths of her solitary auditor to its massive foundations. Then she stopped and asked quietly, "Where is Bob?"

The hermit started. He would look for her. But Bob, for some reason, was not forthcoming. Search was made within and without the hut, but in vain. For the first time that evening Miss

Portfire showed some anxiety. "Go," she said to Barker, "and find her. She *must* be found; stay, give me your overcoat, I'll go myself." She threw the overcoat over her shoulders and stepped out into the night. In the thick veil of fog that seemed suddenly to inwrap her, she stood for a moment irresolute, and then walked toward the beach, guided by the low wash of waters on the sand. She had not taken many steps before she stumbled over some dark crouching object. Reaching down her hand she felt the coarse wiry mane of the Princess.

"Bob!"

There was no reply.

"Bob. I've been looking for you, come."

"Go 'way."

"Nonsense, Bob. I want you to stay with me to-night, come."

"Injin squaw no good for waugee woman. Go 'way."

"Listen, Bob. You are daughter of a chief: so am I. Your father had many warriors: so has mine. It is good that you stay with me. Come."

The Princess chuckled and suffered herself to be lifted up. A few moments later and they re-entered the hut, hand in hand.

With the first red streaks of dawn the next day the erect Barker touched his cap at the door of the hut. Beside him stood the hermit, also just

risen from his blanketed nest in the sand.   Forth
from the hut, fresh as the morning air, stepped
Miss Portfire, leading the Princess by the hand.
Hand in hand also they walked to the shore, and
when the Princess had been safely bestowed in
the stern sheets, Miss Portfire turned and held out
her own to her late host.

"I shall take the best of care of her, of course.
You will come and see her often. I should ask
you to come and see me, but you are a hermit,
you know, and all that sort of thing.   But if it's
the correct anchorite thing, and can be done, my
father will be glad to requite you for this night's
hospitality.   But don't do anything on my account
that interferes with your simple habits.   Good
by."

She handed him a card, which he took mechanically.

"Good by."

The sail was hoisted, and the boat shoved off.
As the fresh morning breeze caught the white canvas it seemed to bow a parting salutation.   There
was a rosy flush of promise on the water, and as
the light craft darted forward toward the ascending sun, it seemed for a moment uplifted in its
glory.

Miss Portfire kept her word.   If thoughtful
care and intelligent kindness could regenerate the

Princess, her future was secure. And it really seemed as if she were for the first time inclined to heed the lessons of civilization and profit by her new condition. An agreeable change was first noticed in her appearance. Her lawless hair was caught in a net, and no longer strayed over her low forehead. Her unstable bust was stayed and upheld by French corsets; her plantigrade shuffle was limited by heeled boots. Her dresses were neat and clean, and she wore a double necklace of glass beads. With this physical improvement there also seemed some moral awakening. She no longer stole nor lied. With the possession of personal property came a respect for that of others. With increased dependence on the word of those about her came a thoughtful consideration of her own. Intellectually she was still feeble, although she grappled sturdily with the simple lessons which Miss Portfire set before her. But her zeal and simple vanity outran her discretion, and she would often sit for hours with an open book before her, which she could not read. She was a favorite with the officers at the fort, from the Major, who shared his daughter's prejudices and often yielded to her powerful self-will, to the subalterns, who liked her none the less that their natural enemies, the frontier volunteers, had declared war against her helpless sisterhood. The only restraint put upon her was the limitation of her liberty to the enclosure of the fort and parade; and only once did she break this parole, and was stopped by the sentry as she stepped into a boat at the landing.

The recluse did not avail himself of Miss Portfire's invitation. But after the departure of the Princess he spent less of his time in the hut, and was more frequently seen in the distant marshes of Eel River and on the upland hills. A feverish restlessness, quite opposed to his usual phlegm, led him into singular freaks strangely inconsistent with his usual habits and reputation. The purser of the occasional steamer which stopped at Logport with the mails reported to have been boarded, just inside the bar, by a strange bearded man, who asked for a newspaper containing the last war telegrams. He tore his red shirt into narrow strips, and spent two days with his needle over the pieces and the tattered remnant of his only white garment; and a few days afterward the fishermen on the bay were surprised to see what, on nearer approach, proved to be a rude imitation of the national flag floating from a spar above the hut.

One evening, as the fog began to drift over the sand-hills, the recluse sat alone in his hut. The fire was dying unheeded on the hearth, for he had been sitting there for a long time, completely absorbed in the blurred pages of an old newspaper.

Presently he arose, and, refolding it, — an operation of great care and delicacy in its tattered condition, — placed it under the blankets of his bed. He resumed his seat by the fire, but soon began drumming with his fingers on the arm of his chair. Eventually this assumed the time and accent of some air. Then he began to whistle softly and hesitatingly, as if trying to recall a forgotten tune. Finally this took shape in a rude resemblance, not unlike that which his flag bore to the national standard, to Yankee Doodle. Suddenly he stopped.

There was an unmistakable rapping at the door. The blood which had at first rushed to his face now forsook it and settled slowly around his heart. He tried to rise, but could not. Then the door was flung open, and a figure with a scarlet-lined hood and fur mantle stood on the threshold. With a mighty effort he took one stride to the door. The next moment he saw the wide mouth and white teeth of the Princess, and was greeted by a kiss that felt like a baptism.

To tear the hood and mantle from her figure in the sudden fury that seized him, and to fiercely demand the reason of this masquerade, was his only return to her greeting. " Why are you here? did you steal these garments?" he again demanded in her guttural language, as he shook her roughly by the arm. The Princess hung her head. "Did you ?" he screamed, as he reached wildly for his rifle.

"I did."

His hold relaxed, and he staggered back against the wall. The Princess began to whimper. Between her sobs, she was trying to explain that the Major and his daughter were going away, and that they wanted to send her to the Reservation; but he cut her short. "Take off those things!" The Princess tremblingly obeyed. He rolled them up, placed them in the canoe she had just left, and then leaped into the frail craft. She would have followed, but with a great oath he threw her from him, and with one stroke of his paddle swept out into the fog, and was gone.

"Jessamy," said the Major, a few days after, as he sat at dinner with his daughter, "I think I can tell you something to match the mysterious disappearance and return of your wardrobe. Your crazy friend, the recluse, has enlisted this morning in the Fourth Artillery. He's a splendid-looking animal, and there's the right stuff for a soldier in him, if I'm not mistaken. He's in earnest too, for he enlists in the regiment ordered back to Washington. Bless me, child, another goblet broken; you'll ruin the mess in glassware, at this rate!"

"Have you heard anything more of the Princess, papa?"

"Nothing, but perhaps it's as well that she has gone. These cursed settlers are at their old complaints again about what they call 'Indian depredations,' and I have just received orders from head-quarters to keep the settlement clear of all vagabond aborigines. I am afraid, my dear, that a strict construction of the term would include your *protégée*."

The time for the departure of the Fourth Artillery had come. The night before was thick and foggy. At one o'clock, a shot on the ramparts called out the guard and roused the sleeping garrison. The new sentry, Private Grey, had challenged a dusky figure creeping on the glacis, and, receiving no answer, had fired. The guard sent out presently returned, bearing a lifeless figure in their arms. The new sentry's zeal, joined with an ex-frontiersman's aim, was fatal.

They laid the helpless, ragged form before the guard-house door, and then saw for the first time that it was the Princess. Presently she opened her eyes. They fell upon the agonized face of her innocent slayer, but haply without intelligence or reproach.

"Georgy!" she whispered.

"Bob!"

"All's same now. Me get plenty well soon. Me make no more fuss. Me go to Reservation."

Then she stopped, a tremor ran through her limbs, and she lay still. She had gone to the Reservation. Not that devised by the wisdom of man, but that one set apart from the foundation of the world for the wisest as well as the meanest of His creatures.

THE ILIAD OF SANDY BAR.

BEFORE nine o'clock it was pretty well known all along the river that the two partners of the " Amity Claim " had quarrelled and separated at daybreak. At that time the attention of their nearest neighbor had been attracted by the sounds of altercations and two consecutive pistol-shots. Running out, he had seen, dimly, in the gray mist that rose from the river, the tall form of Scott, one of the partners, descending the hill toward the *cañon;* a moment later, York, the other partner, had appeared from the cabin, and walked in an opposite direction toward the river, passing within a few feet of the curious watcher. Later it was discovered that a serious Chinaman, cutting wood before the cabin, had witnessed part of the quarrel. But John was stolid, indifferent, and reticent. "Me choppee wood, me no fightee," was his serene response to all anxious queries. " But what did they *say,* John ? " John did not *sabe.* Colonel Starbottle deftly ran over the various popular epithets which a generous public sentiment might accept as reasonable provocation for an assault. But John did not recognize them. "And this yer's the cat-

tle," said the Colonel, with some severity, "that
some thinks oughter be allowed to testify ag'in' a
White Man! Git — you heathen !"

Still the quarrel remained inexplicable. That
two men, whose amiability and grave tact had
earned for them the title of "The Peacemakers,"
in a community not greatly given to the passive virtues, — that these men, singularly devoted to each
other, should suddenly and violently quarrel, might
well excite the curiosity of the camp. A few
of the more inquisitive visited the late scene of
conflict, now deserted by its former occupants.
There was no trace of disorder or confusion in the
neat cabin. The rude table was arranged as if
for breakfast; the pan of yellow biscuit still sat
upon that hearth whose dead embers might have
typified the evil passions that had raged there
but an hour before. But Colonel Starbottle's eye
— albeit somewhat bloodshot and rheumy — was
more intent on practical details. On examination,
a bullet-hole was found in the doorpost, and
another, nearly opposite, in the casing of the window. The Colonel called attention to the fact that
the one "agreed with" the bore of Scott's revolver,
and the other with that of York's derringer.
"They must hev stood about yer," said the Colonel, taking position; "not mor'n three feet apart,
and — missed !" There was a fine touch of pathos
in the falling inflection of the Colonel's voice,

which was not without effect. A delicate perception of wasted opportunity thrilled his auditors.

But the Bar was destined to experience a greater disappointment. The two antagonists had not met since the quarrel, and it was vaguely rumored that, on the occasion of a second meeting, each had determined to kill the other " on sight." There was, consequently, some excitement — and, it is to be feared, no little gratification — when, at ten o'clock, York stepped from the Magnolia Saloon into the one long straggling street of the camp, at the same moment that Scott left the blacksmith's shop at the forks of the road. It was evident, at a glance, that a meeting could only be avoided by the actual retreat of one or the other.

In an instant the doors and windows of the adjacent saloons were filled with faces. Heads unaccountably appeared above the river-banks and from behind bowlders. An empty wagon at the cross-road was suddenly crowded with people, who seemed to have sprung from the earth. There was much running and confusion on the hillside. On the mountain-road, Mr. Jack Hamlin had reined up his horse, and was standing upright on the seat of his buggy. And the two objects of this absorbing attention approached each other.

"York's got the sun," "Scott'll line him on that

tree," " He's waitin' to draw his fire," came from the cart; and then it was silent. But above this human breathlessness the river rushed and sang, and the wind rustled the tree-tops with an indifference that seemed obtrusive. Colonel Starbottle felt it, and in a moment of sublime preoccupation, without looking around, waved his cane behind him, warningly to all nature, and said, " Shu!"

The men were now within a few feet of each other. A hen ran across the road before one of them. A feathery seed-vessel, wafted from a wayside tree, fell at the feet of the other. And, unheeding this irony of nature, the two opponents came nearer, erect and rigid, looked in each other's eyes, and — passed!

Colonel Starbottle had to be lifted from the cart. " This yer camp is played out," he said, gloomily, as he affected to be supported into the Magnolia. With what further expression he might have indicated his feelings it was impossible to say, for at that moment Scott joined the group. " Did you speak to me ?" he asked of the Colonel, dropping his hand, as if with accidental familiarity, on that gentleman's shoulder. The Colonel, recognizing some occult quality in the touch, and some unknown quantity in the glance of his questioner, contented himself by replying, " No, sir," with dignity. A few rods away, York's conduct was as characteristic and peculiar. "You had a mighty fine chance; why did n't you plump him?" said Jack Hamlin, as York drew near the buggy. "Because I hate him," was the reply, heard only by Jack. Contrary to popular belief, this reply was not hissed between the lips of the speaker, but was said in an ordinary tone. But Jack Hamlin, who was an observer of mankind, noticed that the speaker's hands were cold, and his lips dry, as he helped him into the buggy, and accepted the seeming paradox with a smile.

When Sandy Bar became convinced that the quarrel between York and Scott could not be settled after the usual local methods, it gave no further concern thereto. But presently it was rumored that the "Amity Claim" was in litigation, and that its possession would be expensively disputed by each of the partners. As it was well known that the claim in question was "worked out" and worthless, and that the partners, whom it had already enriched, had talked of abandoning it but a day or two before the quarrel, this proceeding could only be accounted for as gratuitous spite. Later, two San Francisco lawyers made their appearance in this guileless Arcadia, and were eventually taken into the saloons, and — what was pretty much the same thing — the confidences of the inhabitants. The results of this unhallowed intimacy were many subpœnas ; and, indeed, when the "Amity Claim" came to trial, all of Sandy Bar that was not in compulsory attendance at the county seat came there from curiosity. The gulches and ditches for miles around were deserted. I do not propose to describe that already famous trial. Enough that, in the language of the plaintiff's counsel, "it was one of no ordinary significance, involving the inherent rights of that untiring industry which had developed the Pactolian resources of this golden land"; and, in the homelier phrase of Colonel Starbottle, "A fuss that gentlemen might hev settled in ten minutes over a social glass, ef they meant business ; or in ten seconds with a revolver, ef they meant fun." Scott got a verdict, from which York instantly appealed. It was said that he had sworn to spend his last dollar in the struggle.

In this way Sandy Bar began to accept the enmity of the former partners as a lifelong feud, and the fact that they had ever been friends was forgotten. The few who expected to learn from the trial the origin of the quarrel were disappointed. Among the various conjectures, that which ascribed some occult feminine influence as the cause was naturally popular, in a camp given to dubious compliment of the sex. "My word for it, gentlemen," said Colonel Starbottle, who had been known in Sacramento as a Gentleman of the

Old School, "there's some lovely creature at the bottom of this." The gallant Colonel then proceeded to illustrate his theory, by divers sprightly stories, such as Gentlemen of the Old School are in the habit of repeating, but which, from deference to the prejudices of gentlemen of a more recent school, I refrain from transcribing here. But it would appear that even the Colonel's theory was fallacious. The only woman who personally might have exercised any influence over the partners was the pretty daughter of "old man Folinsbee," of Poverty Flat, at whose hospitable house — which exhibited some comforts and refinements rare in that crude civilization — both York and Scott were frequent visitors. Yet into this charming retreat York strode one evening, a month after the quarrel, and, beholding Scott sitting there, turned to the fair hostess with the abrupt query, "Do you love this man?" The young woman thus addressed returned that answer — at once spirited and evasive — which would occur to most of my fair readers in such an exigency. Without another word, York left the house. "Miss Jo" heaved the least possible sigh as the door closed on York's curls and square shoulders, and then, like a good girl, turned to her insulted guest. "But would you believe it, dear?" she afterward related to an intimate friend, "the other creature, after glowering at me for a moment, got upon its hind legs, took its hat, and left, too; and that's the last I 've seen of either."

The same hard disregard of all other interests or feelings in the gratification of their blind rancor characterized all their actions. When York purchased the land below Scott's new claim, and obliged the latter, at a great expense, to make a long détour to carry a " tail-race " around it, Scott retaliated by building a dam that overflowed York's claim on the river. It was Scott, who, in conjunction with Colonel Starbottle, first organized that active opposition to the Chinamen, which resulted in the driving off of York's Mongolian laborers; it was York who built the wagon-road and established the express which rendered Scott's mules and pack-trains obsolete; it was Scott who called into life the Vigilance Committee which expatriated York's friend, Jack Hamlin; it was York who created the " Sandy Bar Herald," which characterized the act as " a lawless outrage," and Scott as a " Border Ruffian "; it was Scott, at the head of twenty masked men, who, one moonlight night, threw the offending " forms " into the yellow river, and scattered the types in the dusty road. These proceedings were received in the distant and more civilized outlying towns as vague indications of progress and vitality. I have before me a copy of the " Poverty Flat Pioneer," for the week ending August 12, 1856, in which the editor,

under the head of "County Improvements," says:
"The new Presbyterian Church on C Street, at
Sandy Bar, is completed. It stands upon the lot
formerly occupied by the Magnolia Saloon, which
was so mysteriously burnt last month. The
temple, which now rises like a Phœnix from the
ashes of the Magnolia, is virtually the free gift of
H. J. York, Esq., of Sandy Bar, who purchased
the lot and donated the lumber. Other buildings
are going up in the vicinity, but the most notice-
able is the 'Sunny South Saloon,' erected by Captain Mat. Scott, nearly opposite the church. Captain Scott has spared no expense in the furnishing
of this saloon, which promises to be one of the
most agreeable places of resort in old Tuolumne.
He has recently imported two new, first-class bil-
liard-tables, with cork cushions. Our old friend,
'Mountain Jimmy,' will dispense liquors at the
bar. We refer our readers to the advertisement
in another column. Visitors to Sandy Bar cannot do better than give 'Jimmy' a call." Among
the local items occurred the following: "H. J.
York, Esq., of Sandy Bar, has offered a reward of
$100 for the detection of the parties who hauled
away the steps of the new Presbyterian Church, C
Street, Sandy Bar, during divine service on Sab-
bath evening last. Captain Scott adds another
hundred for the capture of the miscreants who
broke the magnificent plate-glass windows of the

new saloon on the following evening. There is some talk of reorganizing the old Vigilance Committee at Sandy Bar."

When, for many months of cloudless weather, the hard, unwinking sun of Sandy Bar had regularly gone down on the unpacified wrath of these men, there was some talk of mediation. In particular, the pastor of the church to which I have just referred — a sincere, fearless, but perhaps not fully enlightened man — seized gladly upon the occasion of York's liberality to attempt to reunite the former partners. He preached an earnest sermon on the abstract sinfulness of discord and rancor. But the excellent sermons of the Rev. Mr. Daws were directed to an ideal congregation that did not exist at Sandy Bar, — a congregation of beings of unmixed vices and virtues, of single impulses, and perfectly logical motives, of preternatural simplicity, of childlike faith, and grown-up responsibilities. As, unfortunately, the people who actually attended Mr. Daws's church were mainly very human, somewhat artful, more self-excusing than self-accusing, rather good-natured, and decidedly weak, they quietly shed that portion of the sermon which referred to themselves, and, accepting York and Scott — who were both in defiant attendance — as curious examples of those ideal beings above referred to, felt a certain satisfaction — which, I fear, was not altogether Christian-like

— in their "raking-down." If Mr. Daws expected York and Scott to shake hands after the sermon, he was disappointed. But he did not relax his purpose. With that quiet fearlessness and determination which had won for him the respect of men who were too apt to regard piety as synonymous with effeminacy, he attacked Scott in his own house. What he said has not been recorded, but it is to be feared that it was part of his sermon. When he had concluded, Scott looked at him, not unkindly, over the glasses of his bar, and said, less irreverently than the words might convey, "Young man, I rather like your style; but when you know York and me as well as you do God Almighty, it 'll be time to talk."

And so the feud progressed; and so, as in more illustrious examples, the private and personal enmity of two representative men led gradually to the evolution of some crude, half-expressed principle or belief. It was not long before it was made evident that those beliefs were identical with certain broad principles laid down by the founders of the American Constitution, as expounded by the statesmanlike A.; or were the fatal quicksands, on which the ship of state might be wrecked, warningly pointed out by the eloquent B. The practical result of all which was the nomination of York and Scott to represent the opposite factions of Sandy Bar in legislative councils.

For some weeks past, the voters of Sandy Bar and the adjacent camps had been called upon, in large type, to "RALLY !"   In vain the great pines at the cross-roads — whose trunks were compelled to bear this and other legends — moaned and protested from their windy watch-towers.   But one day, with fife and drum, and flaming transparency, a procession filed into the triangular grove at the head of the gulch.   The meeting was called to order by Colonel Starbottle, who, having once enjoyed legislative functions, and being vaguely known as a "war-horse," was considered to be a valuable partisan of York.   He concluded an appeal for his friend, with an enunciation of principles, interspersed with one or two anecdotes so gratuitously coarse that the very pines might have been moved to pelt him with their cast-off cones, as he stood there.   But he created a laugh, on which his candidate rode into popular notice; and when York rose to speak, he was greeted with cheers.   But, to the general astonishment, the new speaker at once launched into bitter denunciation of his rival.   He not only dwelt upon Scott's deeds and example, as known to Sandy Bar, but spoke of facts connected with his previous career, hitherto unknown to his auditors.   To great precision of epithet and directness of statement, the speaker added the fascination of revelation and exposure. The crowd cheered, yelled, and were delighted, but when this astounding philippic was concluded, there was a unanimous call for "Scott!" Colonel Starbottle would have resisted, this manifest impropriety, but in vain. Partly from a crude sense of justice, partly from a meaner craving for excitement, the assemblage was inflexible; and Scott was dragged, pushed, and pulled upon the platform.

As his frowsy head and unkempt beard appeared above the railing, it was evident that he was drunk. But it was also evident, before he opened his lips, that the orator of Sandy Bar — the one man who could touch their vagabond sympathies (perhaps because he was not above appealing to them) — stood before them. A consciousness of this power lent a certain dignity to his figure, and I am not sure but that his very physical condition impressed them as a kind of regal unbending and large condescension. Howbeit, when this unexpected Hector arose from the ditch, York's myrmidons trembled.

"There's naught, gentlemen," said Scott, leaning forward on the railing, — "there's naught as that man hez said as is n't true. I was run outer Cairo; I did belong to the Regulators; I did desert from the army; I did leave a wife in Kansas. But thar's one thing he did n't charge me with, and, maybe, he's forgotten. For three years, gentlemen, I was that man's pardner!—" Whether he intended to say more, I cannot tell; a burst of applause artistically rounded and enforced the climax, and virtually elected the speaker. That fall he went to Sacramento, York went abroad; and for the first time in many years, distance and a new atmosphere isolated the old antagonists.

With little of change in the green wood, gray rock, and yellow river, but with much shifting of human landmarks, and new faces in its habitations, three years passed over Sandy Bar. The two men, once so identified with its character, seemed to have been quite forgotten. "You will never return to Sandy Bar," said Miss Folinsbee, the " Lily of Poverty Flat," on meeting York in Paris, "for Sandy Bar is no more. They call it Riverside now; and the new town is built higher up on the river-bank. By the by, 'Jo' says that Scott has won his suit about the 'Amity Claim,' and that he lives in the old cabin, and is drunk half his time. O, I beg your pardon," added the lively lady, as a flush crossed York's sallow cheek; " but, bless me, I really thought that old grudge was made up. I 'm sure it ought to be."

It was three months after this conversation, and a pleasant summer evening, that the Poverty Flat coach drew up before the veranda of the Union Hotel at Sandy Bar. Among its passengers was one, apparently a stranger, in the local distinction

of well-fitting clothes and closely shaven face, who
demanded a private room and retired early to rest.
But before sunrise next morning he arose, and,
drawing some clothes from his carpet-bag, proceeded to array himself in a pair of white duck
trousers, a white duck overshirt, and straw hat.
When his toilet was completed, he tied a red ban-
danna handkerchief in a loop and threw it loosely
over his shoulders. The transformation was complete. As he crept softly down the stairs and
stepped into the road, no one would have detected
in him the elegant stranger of the previous night,
and but few have recognized the face and figure of
Henry York of Sandy Bar.

In the uncertain light of that early hour, and in
the change that had come over the settlement, he
had to pause for a moment to recall where he
stood. The Sandy Bar of his recollection lay below him, nearer the river; the buildings around
him were of later date and newer fashion. As he
strode toward the river, he noticed here a school-
house and there a church. A little farther on,
"The Sunny South" came in view, transformed
into a restaurant, its gilding faded and its paint
rubbed off. He now knew where he was; and,
running briskly down a declivity, crossed a ditch,
and stood upon the lower boundary of the Amity
Claim.

The gray mist was rising slowly from the river,

clinging to the tree-tops and drifting up the mountain-side, until it was caught among those rocky altars, and held a sacrifice to the ascending sun. At his feet the earth, cruelly gashed and scarred by his forgotten engines, had, since the old days, put on a show of greenness here and there, and now smiled forgivingly up at him, as if things were not so bad after all. A few birds were bathing in the ditch with a pleasant suggestion of its being a new and special provision of nature, and a hare ran into an inverted sluice-box, as he approached, as if it were put there for that purpose.

He had not yet dared to look in a certain direction. But the sun was now high enough to paint the little eminence on which the cabin stood. In spite of his self-control, his heart beat faster as he raised his eyes toward it. Its window and door were closed, no smoke came from its *adobe* chimney, but it was else unchanged. When within a few yards of it, he picked up a broken shovel, and, shouldering it with a smile, strode toward the door and knocked. There was no sound from within. The smile died upon his lips as he nervously pushed the door open.

A figure started up angrily and came toward him, — a figure whose bloodshot eyes suddenly fixed into a vacant stare, whose arms were at first outstretched and then thrown up in warning gesticulation, — a figure that suddenly gasped, choked, and then fell forward in a fit.

But before he touched the ground, York had him out into the open air and sunshine. In the struggle, both fell and rolled over on the ground. But the next moment York was sitting up, holding the convulsed frame of his former partner on his knee, and wiping the foam from his inarticulate lips. Gradually the tremor became less frequent, and then ceased; and the strong man lay unconscious in his arms.

For some moments York held him quietly thus, looking in his face. Afar, the stroke of a woodman's axe — a mere phantom of sound — was all that broke the stillness. High up the mountain, a wheeling hawk hung breathlessly above them. And then came voices, and two men joined them.

"A fight?" No, a fit; and would they help him bring the sick man to the hotel?

And there, for a week, the stricken partner lay, unconscious of aught but the visions wrought by disease and fear. On the eighth day, at sunrise, he rallied, and, opening his eyes, looked upon York, and pressed his hand; then he spoke: —

"And it's you. I thought it was only whiskey."

York replied by taking both of his hands, boyishly working them backward and forward, as his elbow rested on the bed, with a pleasant smile.

" And you 've been abroad.   How did you like Paris ? "

" So, so.   How did *you* like Sacramento ? "

" Bully."

And that was all they could think to say. Presently Scott opened his eyes again.

" I 'm mighty weak."

" You 'll get better soon."

" Not much."

A long silence followed, in which they could hear the sounds of wood-chopping, and that Sandy Bar was already astir for the coming day.   Then Scott slowly and with difficulty turned his face to York, and said, —

" I might hev killed you once."

" I wish you had."

They pressed each other's hands again, but Scott's grasp was evidently failing.   He seemed to summon his energies for a special effort.

" Old man ! "

" Old chap."

" Closer ! "

York bent his head toward the slowly fading face.

" Do ye mind that morning ? "

" Yes."

A gleam of fun slid into the corner of Scott's blue eye, as he whispered, —

" Old man, thar *was* too much saleratus in that bread."

It is said that these were his last words. For when the sun, which had so often gone down upon the idle wrath of these foolish men, looked again upon them reunited, it saw the hand of Scott fall cold and irresponsive from the yearning clasp of his former partner, and it knew that the feud of Sandy Bar was at an end.

MR. THOMPSON'S PRODIGAL

WE all knew that Mr. Thompson was looking for his son, and a pretty bad one at that. That he was coming to California for this sole object was no secret to his fellow-passengers ; and the physical peculiarities, as well as the moral weaknesses, of the missing prodigal were made equally plain to us through the frank volubility of the parent. "You was speaking of a young man which was hung at Red Dog for sluice-robbing," said Mr. Thompson to a steerage passenger, one day ; "be you aware of the color of his eyes ?" "Black," responded the passenger. "Ah," said Mr. Thompson, referring to some mental memoranda, "Char-les's eyes was blue." He then walked away. Perhaps it was from this unsympathetic mode of inquiry, perhaps it was from that Western predilection to take a humorous view of any principle or sentiment persistently brought before them, that Mr. Thompson's quest was the subject of some satire among the passengers. A gratuitous advertisement of the missing Charles, addressed to "Jailers and Guardians," circulated privately among them ; everybody remembered to have met

Charles under distressing circumstances.   Yet
it is but due to my countrymen to state that
when it was known that Thompson had embarked
some wealth in this visionary project, but little of
this satire found its way to his ears, and nothing
was uttered in his hearing that might bring a pang
to a father's heart, or imperil a possible pecuniary
advantage of the satirist.   Indeed, Mr. Bracy
Tibbets's jocular proposition to form a joint-stock
company to "prospect" for the missing youth received at one time quite serious entertainment.

Perhaps to superficial criticism Mr. Thompson's
nature was not picturesque nor lovable.   His history, as imparted at dinner, one day, by himself,
was practical even in its singularity.   After a hard
and wilful youth and maturity, — in which he
had buried a broken-spirited wife, and driven his
son to sea, — he suddenly experienced religion.   " I
got it in New Orleans in '59," said Mr. Thompson,
with the general suggestion of referring to an epidemic.   " Enter ye the narrer gate.   Parse me the
beans."   Perhaps this practical quality upheld him
in his apparently hopeless search.   He had no
clew to the whereabouts of his runaway son; indeed, scarcely a proof of his present existence.
From his indifferent recollection of the boy of
twelve, he now expected to identify the man of
twenty-five.

It would seem that he was successful.   How he

succeeded was one of the few things he did not
tell. There are, I believe, two versions of the
story. One, that Mr. Thompson, visiting a hospital, discovered his son by reason of a peculiar
hymn, chanted by the sufferer, in a delirious dream
of his boyhood. This version, giving as it did
wide range to the finer feelings of the heart, was
quite popular; and as told by the Rev. Mr. Gush-
ington, on his return from his California tour,
never failed to satisfy an audience. The other was
less simple, and, as I shall adopt it here, deserves
more elaboration.

It was after Mr. Thompson had given up searching for his son among the living, and had taken
to the examination of cemeteries, and a careful in-
spection of the " cold *hic jacets* of the dead." At
this time he was a frequent visitor of " Lone
Mountain," — a dreary hill-top, bleak enough in
its original isolation, and bleaker for the white-
faced marbles by which San Francisco anchored
her departed citizens, and kept them down in a
shifting sand that refused to cover them, and
against a fierce and persistent wind that strove to
blow them utterly away. Against this wind the
old man opposed a will quite as persistent, — a
grizzled, hard face, and a tall, crape-bound hat
drawn tightly over his eyes, — and so spent days
in reading the mortuary inscriptions audibly to
himself. The frequency of Scriptural quotation

pleased him, and he was fond of corroborating them by a pocket Bible. "That's from Psalms," he said, one day, to an adjacent grave-digger. The man made no reply. Not at all rebuffed, Mr. Thompson at once slid down into the open grave, with a more practical inquiry, "Did you ever, in your profession, come across Char-les Thompson?" "Thompson be d—d!" said the grave-digger, with great directness. "Which, if he had n't religion, I think he is," responded the old man, as he clambered out of the grave.

It was, perhaps, on this occasion that Mr. Thompson stayed later than usual. As he turned his face toward the city, lights were beginning to twinkle ahead, and a fierce wind, made visible by fog, drove him forward, or, lying in wait, charged him angrily from the corners of deserted suburban streets. It was on one of these corners that something else, quite as indistinct and malevolent, leaped upon him with an oath, a presented pistol, and a demand for money. But it was met by a will of iron and a grip of steel. The assailant and assailed rolled together on the ground. But the next moment the old man was erect; one hand grasping the captured pistol, the other clutching at arm's length the throat of a figure, surly, youthful, and savage.

"Young man," said Mr. Thompson, setting his thin lips together, "what might be your name?"

"Thompson!"

The old man's hand slid from the throat to the arm of his prisoner, without relaxing its firmness.

"Char-les Thompson, come with me," he said, presently, and marched his captive to the hotel. What took place there has not transpired, but it was known the next morning that Mr. Thompson had found his son.

It is proper to add to the above improbable story, that there was nothing in the young man's appearance or manners to justify it. Grave, reticent, and handsome, devoted to his newly found parent, he assumed the emoluments and responsibilities of his new condition with a certain serious ease that more nearly approached that which San Francisco society lacked, and — rejected. Some chose to despise this quality as a tendency to "psalm-singing"; others saw in it the inherited qualities of the parent, and were ready to prophesy for the son the same hard old age. But all agreed that it was not inconsistent with the habits of money-getting, for which father and son were respected.

And yet, the old man did not seem to be happy. Perhaps it was that the consummation of his wishes left him without a practical mission; perhaps — and it is the more probable — he had little love for the son he had regained. The obedience he exacted was freely given, the reform he had set his heart upon was complete; and yet, somehow, it did not seem to please him. In reclaiming his son, he had fulfilled all the requirements that his religious duty required of him, and yet the act seemed to lack sanctification. In this perplexity, he read again the parable of the Prodigal Son, — which he had long ago adopted for his guidance, — and found that he had omitted the final feast of reconciliation. This seemed to offer the proper quality of ceremoniousness in the sacrament between himself and his son; and so, a year after the appearance of Charles, he set about giving him a party. "Invite everybody, Char-les," he said, dryly; "everybody who knows that I brought you out of the wine-husks of iniquity, and the company of harlots; and bid them eat, drink, and be merry."

Perhaps the old man had another reason, not yet clearly analyzed. The fine house he had built on the sand-hills sometimes seemed lonely and bare. He often found himself trying to reconstruct, from the grave features of Charles, the little boy whom he but dimly remembered in the past, and of whom lately he had been thinking a great deal. He believed this to be a sign of impending old age and childishness; but coming, one day, in his formal drawing-room, upon a child of one of the servants, who had strayed therein, he would

have taken him in his arms, but the child fled from
before his grizzled face. So that it seemed emi-
nently proper to invite a number of people to his
house, and, from the array of San Francisco maid-
enhood, to select a daughter-in-law. And then
there would be a child — a boy, whom he could
"rare up" from the beginning, and — love — as
he did not love Charles.

We were all at the party. The Smiths, Joneses,
Browns, and Robinsons also came, in that fine flow
of animal spirits, unchecked by any respect for the
entertainer, which most of us are apt to find so
fascinating. The proceedings would have been
somewhat riotous, but for the social position of
the actors. In fact, Mr. Bracy Tibbets, having
naturally a fine appreciation of a humorous situation, but further impelled by the bright eyes of the
Jones girls, conducted himself so remarkably as to
attract the serious regard of Mr. Charles Thompson, who approached him, saying quietly: "You
look ill, Mr. Tibbets; let me conduct you to your
carriage. Resist, you hound, and I'll throw you
through that window. This way, please; the room
is close and distressing." It is hardly necessary to
say that but a part of this speech was audible to
the company, and that the rest was not divulged
by Mr. Tibbets, who afterward regretted the sudden illness which kept him from witnessing a certain amusing incident, which the fastest Miss Jones

characterized as the " richest part of the blow-out," and which I hasten to record.

It was at supper. It was evident that Mr. Thompson had overlooked much lawlessness in the conduct of the younger people, in his abstract contemplation of some impending event. When the cloth was removed, he rose to his feet, and grimly tapped upon the table. A titter, that broke out among the Jones girls, became epidemic on one side of the board. Charles Thompson, from the foot of the table, looked up in tender perplexity. " He's going to sing a Doxology," " He's going to pray," "Silence for a speech," ran round the room.

" It's one year to-day, Christian brothers and sisters," said Mr. Thompson, with grim deliberation, — " one year to-day since my son came home from eating of wine-husks and spending of his substance on harlots." (The tittering suddenly ceased.) "Look at him now. Char-les Thompson, stand up." (Charles Thompson stood up.) " One year ago to-day, — and look at him now."

He was certainly a handsome prodigal, standing there in his cheerful evening-dress, — a repentant prodigal, with sad, obedient eyes turned upon the harsh and unsympathetic glance of his father. The youngest Miss Smith, from the pure depths of her foolish little heart, moved unconsciously toward him.

" It's fifteen years ago since he left my house,"
said Mr. Thompson, " a rovier and a prodigal. I
was myself a man of sin, O Christian friends, — a
man of wrath and bitterness" (" Amen," from
the eldest Miss Smith), — " but praise be God, I've
fled the wrath to come. It's five years ago since
I got the peace that passeth understanding. Have
you got it, friends ? " (A general sub-chorus of
" No, no," from the girls, and, " Pass the word for
it," from Midshipman Coxe, of the U. S. sloop
Wethersfield.) " Knock, and it shall be opened to
you.

" And when I found the error of my ways, and
the preciousness of grace," continued Mr. Thompson, " I came to give it to my son. By sea and
land I sought him far, and fainted not. I did not
wait for him to come to me, which the same I
might have done, and justified myself by the Book
of books, but I sought him out among his husks,
and — " (the rest of the sentence was lost in the
rustling withdrawal of the ladies). " Works,
Christian friends, is my motto. By their works
shall ye know them, and there is mine."

The particular and accepted work to which Mr.
Thompson was alluding had turned quite pale, and
was looking fixedly toward an open door leading
to the veranda, lately filled by gaping servants,
and now the scene of some vague tumult. As the
noise continued, a man, shabbily dressed, and evi-

dently in liquor, broke through the opposing guardians, and staggered into the room. The transition from the fog and darkness without to the glare and heat within evidently dazzled and stupefied him. He removed his battered hat, and passed it once or twice before his eyes, as he steadied himself, but unsuccessfully, by the back of a chair. Suddenly, his wandering glance fell upon the pale face of Charles Thompson; and with a gleam of childlike recognition, and a weak, falsetto laugh, he darted forward, caught at the table, upset the glasses, and literally fell upon the prodigal's breast.

"Sha'ly ! yo' d—d ol' scoun'rel, hoo rar ye !"

"Hush !— sit down !— hush !" said Charles Thompson, hurriedly endeavoring to extricate himself from the embrace of his unexpected guest.

"Look at 'm !" continued the stranger, unheeding the admonition, but suddenly holding the unfortunate Charles at arm's length, in loving and undisguised admiration of his festive appearance. "Look at 'm ! Ain't he nasty ? Sha'ls, I 'm prow of yer !"

"Leave the house !" said Mr. Thompson, rising, with a dangerous look in his cold, gray eye. "Char-les, how dare you ?"

"Simmer down, ole man ! Sha'ls, who 's th' ol' bloat ? Eh ?"

"Hush, man : here, take this !" With nervous

hands, Charles Thompson filled a glass with liquor. "Drink it and go — until to-morrow — any time, but — leave us ! — go now !" But even then, ere the miserable wretch could drink, the old man, pale with passion, was upon him. Half carrying him in his powerful arms, half dragging him through the circling crowd of frightened guests, he had reached the door, swung open by the waiting servants, when Charles Thompson started from a seeming stupor, crying, —

"Stop !"

The old man stopped. Through the open door the fog and wind drove chilly. "What does this mean ?" he asked, turning a baleful face on Charles.

"Nothing — but stop — for God's sake. Wait till to-morrow, but not to-night. Do not — I implore you — do this thing."

There was something in the tone of the young man's voice, something, perhaps, in the contact of the struggling wretch he held in his powerful arms ; but a dim, indefinite fear took possession of the old man's heart. "Who," he whispered, hoarsely, "is this man ?"

Charles did not answer.

"Stand back, there, all of you," thundered Mr. Thompson, to the crowding guests around him. "Char-les — come here ! I command you — I — I — I — beg you — tell me *who* is this man ?"

Only two persons heard the answer that came faintly from the lips of Charles Thompson, —

"YOUR SON."

When day broke over the bleak sand-hills, the guests had departed from Mr. Thompson's banquet-halls. The lights still burned dimly and coldly in the deserted rooms, — deserted by all but three figures, that huddled together in the chill drawing-room, as if for warmth. One lay in drunken slumber on a couch; at his feet sat he who had been known as Charles Thompson; and beside them, haggard and shrunken to half his size, bowed the figure of Mr. Thompson, his gray eye fixed, his elbows upon his knees, and his hands clasped over his ears, as if to shut out the sad, entreating voice that seemed to fill the room.

"God knows I did not set about to wilfully deceive. The name I gave that night was the first that came into my thought, — the name of one whom I thought dead, — the dissolute companion of my shame. And when you questioned further, I used the knowledge that I gained from him to touch your heart to set me free; only, I swear, for that! But when you told me who you were, and I first saw the opening of another life before me — then — then — O, sir, if I was hungry, homeless, and reckless, when I would have robbed you of your gold, I was heart-sick, helpless, and desperate, when I would have robbed you of your love!"

The old man stirred not. From his luxurious couch the newly found prodigal snored peacefully.

" I had no father I could claim. I never knew a home but this. I was tempted. I have been happy, — very happy."

He rose and stood before the old man.

"Do not fear that I shall come between your son and his inheritance. To-day I leave this place, never to return. The world is large, sir, and, thanks to your kindness, I now see the way by which an honest livelihood is gained. Good by. You will not take my hand? Well, well. Good by."

He turned to go. But when he had reached the door he suddenly came back, and, raising with both hands the grizzled head, he kissed it once and twice.

" Char-les."

There was no reply.

" Char-les!"

The old man rose with a frightened air, and tottered feebly to the door. It was open. There came to him the awakened tumult of a great city, in which the prodigal's footsteps were lost forever.

THE ROMANCE OF MADRONO HOLLOW.

THE latch on the garden gate of the Folinsbee Ranch clicked twice. The gate itself was so much in shadow that lovely night, that "old man Folinsbee," sitting on his porch, could distinguish nothing but a tall white hat and beside it a few fluttering ribbons, under the pines that marked the entrance. Whether because of this fact, or that he considered a sufficient time had elapsed since the clicking of the latch for more positive disclosure, I do not know; but after a few moments' hesitation he quietly laid aside his pipe and walked slowly down the winding path toward the gate. At the Ceanothus hedge he stopped and listened.

There was not much to hear. The hat was saying to the ribbons that it was a fine night, and remarking generally upon the clear outline of the Sierras against the blue-black sky. The ribbons, it so appeared, had admired this all the way home, and asked the hat if it had ever seen anything half so lovely as the moonlight on the summit. The hat never had; it recalled some lovely nights in the South in Alabama ("in the South in Ahla-

bahm " was the way the old man heard it), but
then there were other things that made this night
seem so pleasant.   The ribbons could not possibly
conceive what the hat could be thinking about.   At
this point there was a pause, of which Mr. Folinsbee availed himself to walk very grimly and
craunchingly down the gravel-walk toward the
gate.   Then the hat was lifted, and disappeared in
the shadow, and Mr. Folinsbee confronted only the
half-foolish, half-mischievous, but wholly pretty
face of his daughter.

It was afterward known to Madroño Hollow that
sharp words passed between " Miss Jo " and the old
man, and that the latter coupled the names of one
Culpepper Starbottle and his uncle, Colonel Starbottle, with certain uncomplimentary epithets, and
that Miss Jo retaliated sharply.   " Her father's
blood before her father's face boiled up and proved
her truly of his race," quoted the blacksmith, who
leaned toward the noble verse of Byron.   " She
saw the old man's bluff and raised him," was the
directer comment of the college-bred Masters.

Meanwhile the subject of these animadversions
proceeded slowly along the road to a point where
the Folinsbee mansion came in view, — a long,
narrow, white building, unpretentious, yet superior
to its neighbors, and bearing some evidences of
taste and refinement in the vines that clambered
over its porch, in its French windows, and the

white muslin curtains that kept out the fierce California sun by day, and were now touched with silver in the gracious moonlight. Culpepper leaned against the low fence, and gazed long and earnestly at the building. Then the moonlight vanished ghost-like from one of the windows, a material glow took its place, and a girlish figure, holding a candle, drew the white curtains together. To Culpepper it was a vestal virgin standing before a hallowed shrine ; to the prosaic observer I fear it was only a fair-haired young woman, whose wicked black eyes still shone with unfilial warmth. Howbeit, when the figure had disappeared he stepped out briskly into the moonlight of the high-road. Here he took off his distinguishing hat to wipe his forehead, and the moon shone full upon his face.

It was not an unprepossessing one, albeit a trifle too thin and lank and bilious to be altogether pleasant. The cheek-bones were prominent, and the black eyes sunken in their orbits. Straight black hair fell slantwise off a high but narrow forehead, and swept part of a hollow cheek. A long black mustache followed the perpendicular curves of his mouth. It was on the whole a serious, even Quixotic face, but at times it was relieved by a rare smile of such tender and even pathetic sweetness, that Miss Jo is reported to have said that, if it would only last through the ceremony, she would have married its possessor on the spot.

"I once told him so," added that shameless young woman; "but the man instantly fell into a settled melancholy, and has n't smiled since."

A half-mile below the Folinsbee Ranch the white road dipped and was crossed by a trail that ran through Madroño Hollow. Perhaps because it was a near cut-off to the settlement, perhaps from some less practical reason, Culpepper took this trail, and in a few moments stood among the rarely beautiful trees that gave their name to the valley. Even in that uncertain light the weird beauty of these harlequin masqueraders was apparent; their red trunks — a blush in the moonlight, a deep blood-stain in the shadow — stood out against the silvery green foliage. It was as if Nature in some gracious moment had here caught and crystallized the gypsy memories of the transplanted Spaniard, to cheer him in his lonely exile.

As Culpepper entered the grove he heard loud voices. As he turned toward a clump of trees, a figure so *bizarre* and characteristic that it might have been a resident Daphne — a figure overdressed in crimson silk and lace, with bare brown arms and shoulders, and a wreath of honeysuckle — stepped out of the shadow. It was followed by a man. Culpepper started. To come to the point briefly, he recognized in the man the features of his respected uncle, Colonel Starbottle; in the female, a lady who may be briefly described as one

possessing absolutely no claim to an introduction
to the polite reader. To hurry over equally unpleasant details, both were evidently under the
influence of liquor.

From the excited conversation that ensued, Culpepper gathered that some insult had been put
upon the lady at a public ball which she had attended that evening; that the Colonel, her escort,
had failed to resent it with the sanguinary com-
pleteness that she desired. I regret that, even in
a liberal age, I may not record the exact and even
picturesque language in which this was conveyed
to her hearers. Enough that at the close of a fiery
peroration, with feminine inconsistency she flew at
the gallant Colonel, and would have visited her
delayed vengeance upon his luckless head, but for
the prompt interference of Culpepper. Thwarted
in this, she threw herself upon the ground, and
then into unpicturesque hysterics. There was a
fine moral lesson, not only in this grotesque per-
formance of a sex which cannot afford to be grotesque, but in the ludicrous concern with which
it inspired the two men. Culpepper, to whom
woman was more or less angelic, was pained and
sympathetic; the Colonel, to whom she was more or
less improper, was exceedingly terrified and embarrassed. Howbeit the storm was soon over, and
after Mistress Dolores had returned a little dagger
to its sheath (her garter), she quietly took herself

out of Madroño Hollow, and happily out of these pages forever. The two men, left to themselves, conversed in low tones. Dawn stole upon them before they separated: the Colonel quite sobered and in full possession of his usual jaunty self-assertion; Culpepper with a baleful glow in his hollow cheek, and in his dark eyes a rising fire.

The next morning the general ear of Madroño Hollow was filled with rumors of the Colonel's mishap. It was asserted that he had been invited to withdraw his female companion from the floor of the Assembly Ball at the Independence Hotel, and that, failing to do this, both were expelled. It is to be regretted that in 1854 public opinion was divided in regard to the propriety of this step, and that there was some discussion as to the comparative virtue of the ladies who were not expelled; but it was generally conceded that the real *casus belli* was political. " Is this a dashed Puritan meeting?" had asked the Colonel, savagely. " It's no Pike County shindig," had responded the floor-manager, cheerfully. " You're a Yank!" had screamed the Colonel, profanely qualifying the noun. " Get! you border ruffian," was the reply. Such at least was the substance of the reports. As, at that sincere epoch, expressions like the above were usually followed by prompt action, a fracas was confidently looked for.

Nothing, however, occurred. Colonel Starbottle made his appearance next day upon the streets with somewhat of his usual pomposity, a little restrained by the presence of his nephew, who accompanied him, and who, as a universal favorite, also exercised some restraint upon the curious and impertinent. But Culpepper's face wore a look of anxiety quite at variance with his usual grave repose. "The Don don't seem to take the old man's set-back kindly," observed the sympathizing blacksmith. "P'r'aps he was sweet on Dolores himself," suggested the sceptical expressman.

It was a bright morning, a week after this occurrence, that Miss Jo Folinsbee stepped from her garden into the road. This time the latch did not click as she cautiously closed the gate behind her. After a moment's irresolution, which would have been awkward but that it was charmingly employed, after the manner of her sex, in adjusting a bow under a dimpled but rather prominent chin, and in pulling down the fingers of a neatly fitting glove, she tripped toward the settlement. Small wonder that a passing teamster drove his six mules into the wayside ditch and imperilled his load, to keep the dust from her spotless garments; small wonder that the "Lightning Express" withheld its speed and flash to let her pass, and that the expressman, who had never been known to exchange more than rapid monosyllables with his

fellow-man, gazed after her with breathless admiration. For she was certainly attractive. In a
country where the ornamental sex followed the
example of youthful Nature, and were prone to
overdress and glaring efflorescence, Miss Jo's simple and tasteful raiment added much to the physical charm of, if it did not actually suggest a sentiment to, her presence. It is said that Euchre-deck
Billy, working in the gulch at the crossing, never
saw Miss Folinsbee pass but that he always
remarked apologetically to his partner, that "he
believed he *must* write a letter home." Even Bill
Masters, who saw her in Paris presented to the
favorable criticism of that most fastidious man,
the late Emperor, said that she was stunning, but
a big discount on what she was at Madroño
Hollow.

It was still early morning, but the sun, with
California extravagance, had already begun to beat
hotly on the little chip hat and blue ribbons, and
Miss Jo was obliged to seek the shade of a by-
path. Here she received the timid advances of a
vagabond yellow dog graciously, until, emboldened
by his success, he insisted upon accompanying her,
and, becoming slobberingly demonstrative, threatened her spotless skirt with his dusty paws, when
she drove him from her with some slight acer-
bity, and a stone which haply fell within fifty feet
of its destined mark. Having thus proved her

ability to defend herself, with characteristic inconsistency she took a small panic, and, gathering her
white skirts in one hand, and holding the brim of
her hat over her eyes with the other, she ran
swiftly at least a hundred yards before she stopped.
Then she began picking some ferns and a few
wild-flowers still spared to the withered fields, and
then a sudden distrust of her small ankles seized
her, and she inspected them narrowly for those
burrs and bugs and snakes which are supposed to
lie in wait for helpless womanhood. Then she
plucked some golden heads of wild oats, and with
a sudden inspiration placed them in her black
hair, and then came quite unconsciously upon the
trail leading to Madroño Hollow.

Here she hesitated. Before her ran the little
trail, vanishing at last into the bosky depths below. The sun was very hot. She must be very
far from home. Why should she not rest awhile
under the shade of a madroño ?

She answered these questions by going there at
once. After thoroughly exploring the grove, and
satisfying herself that it contained no other living
human creature, she sat down under one of the
largest trees, with a satisfactory little sigh. Miss
Jo loved the madroño. It was a cleanly tree ; no
dust ever lay upon its varnished leaves ; its im-
maculate shade never was known to harbor grub
or insect.

She looked up at the rosy arms interlocked and arched above her head. She looked down at the delicate ferns and cryptogams at her feet. Something glittered at the root of the tree. She picked it up; it was a bracelet. She examined it carefully for cipher or inscription; there was none. She could not resist a natural desire to clasp it on her arm, and to survey it from that advantageous view-point. This absorbed her attention for some moments; and when she looked up again she beheld at a little distance Culpepper Starbottle.

He was standing where he had halted, with instinctive delicacy, on first discovering her. Indeed, he had even deliberated whether he ought not to go away without disturbing her. But some fascination held him to the spot. Wonderful power of humanity! Far beyond jutted an outlying spur of the Sierra, vast, compact, and silent. Scarcely a hundred yards away, a league-long chasm dropped its sheer walls of granite a thousand feet. On every side rose up the serried ranks of pine-trees, in whose close-set files centuries of storm and change had wrought no breach. Yet all this seemed to Culpepper to have been planned by an all-wise Providence as the natural background to the figure of a pretty girl in a yellow dress.

Although Miss Jo had confidently expected to meet Culpepper somewhere in her ramble, now that he came upon her suddenly, she felt disappointed and embarrassed. His manner, too, was more than usually grave and serious, and more than ever seemed to jar upon that audacious levity which was this giddy girl's power and security in a society where all feeling was dangerous. As he approached her she rose to her feet, but almost before she knew it he had taken her hand and drawn her to a seat beside him. This was not what Miss Jo had expected, but nothing is so difficult to predicate as the exact preliminaries of a declaration of love.

What did Culpepper say? Nothing, I fear, that will add anything to the wisdom of the reader; nothing, I fear, that Miss Jo had not heard substantially from other lips before. But there was a certain conviction, fire-speed, and fury in the manner that was deliciously novel to the young lady. It was certainly something to be courted in the nineteenth century with all the passion and extravagance of the sixteenth; it was something to hear, amid the slang of a frontier society, the language of knight-errantry poured into her ear by this lantern-jawed, dark-browed descendant of the Cavaliers.

I do not know that there was anything more in it. The facts, however, go to show that at a certain point Miss Jo dropped her glove, and that in recovering it Culpepper possessed himself first of her hand and then her lips.   When they stood up to go Culpepper had his arm around her waist, and her black hair, with its sheaf of golden oats, rested against the breast pocket of his coat.   But even then I do not think her fancy was entirely captive. She took a certain satisfaction in this demonstration of Culpepper's splendid height, and mentally compared it with a former flame, one Lieutenant McMirk, an active, but under-sized Hector, who subsequently fell a victim to the incautiously composed and monotonous beverages of a frontier garrison.   Nor was she so much preoccupied but that her quick eyes, even while absorbing Culpepper's glances, were yet able to detect, at a distance, the figure of a man approaching.   In an instant she slipped out of Culpepper's arm, and, whipping her hands behind her, said, " There 's that horrid man ! "

Culpepper looked up and beheld his respected uncle panting and blowing over the hill.   His brow contracted as he turned to Miss Jo : " You don't like my uncle ! "

" I hate him ! "   Miss Jo was recovering her ready tongue.

Culpepper blushed.   He would have liked to enter upon some details of the Colonel's pedigree and exploits, but there was not time.   He only smiled sadly.   The smile melted Miss Jo.   She held out her hand quickly, and said with even more than her usual effrontery, " Don't let that man get you into any trouble. Take care of yourself, dear, and don't let anything happen to you."

Miss Jo intended this speech to be pathetic; the tenure of life among her lovers had hitherto been very uncertain. Culpepper turned toward her, but she had already vanished in the thicket.

The Colonel came up panting. " I 've looked all over town for you, and be dashed to you, sir. Who was that with you ? "

" A lady." (Culpepper never lied, but he was discreet.)

" D—m 'em all ! Look yar, Culp, I 've spotted the man who gave the order to put me off the floor " (" flo " was what the Colonel said) " the other night ! "

" Who was it ? " asked Culpepper, listlessly.

" Jack Folinsbee."

" Who ? "

" Why, the son of that dashed nigger-worship-ping psalm-singing Puritan Yankee. What 's the matter, now ? Look yar, Culp, you ain't goin' back on your blood, ar' ye ? You ain't goin' back on your word ? Ye ain't going down at the feet of this trash, like a whipped hound ? "

Culpepper was silent. He was very white. Presently he looked up and said quietly, " No."

Culpepper Starbottle had challenged Jack Fol-

insbee, and the challenge was accepted.   The cause
alleged was the expelling of Culpepper's uncle from
the floor of the Assembly Ball by the order of
Folinsbee.   This much Madroño Hollow knew and
could swear to; but there were other strange rumors afloat, of which the blacksmith was an able
expounder.   " You see, gentlemen," he said to the
crowd gathered around his anvil, " I ain't got no
theory of this affair, I only give a few facts as have
come to my knowledge.   Culpepper and Jack
meets quite accidental like in Bob's saloon.   Jack
goes up to Culpepper and says, ' A word with you.'
Culpepper bows and steps aside in this way, Jack
standing about *here*."   (The blacksmith demon-
strates the position of the parties with two old
horseshoes on the anvil.)   " Jack pulls a bracelet
from his pocket and says, ' Do you know that
bracelet ? '   Culpepper says, ' I do not,' quite cool-
like and easy.   Jack says, ' You gave it to my sister.'   Culpepper says, still cool as you please, ' I did
not.'   Jack says, ' You lie, G—d d—mn you,' and
draws his derringer.   Culpepper jumps forward
about here " (reference is made to the diagram)
" and Jack fires.   Nobody hit.   It 's a mighty cu-
r'o's thing, gentlemen," continued the blacksmith,
dropping suddenly into the abstract, and leaning
meditatively on his anvil, — " it 's a mighty cur'o's
thing that nobody gets hit so often.   You and me
empties our revolvers sociably at each other over a

little game, and the room full and nobody gets hit!
That's what gets me."

"Never mind, Thompson," chimed in Bill Masters, "there's another and a better world where
we shall know all that and — become better shots.
Go on with your story."

"Well, some grabs Culpepper and some grabs
Jack, and so separates them. Then Jack tells 'em
as how he had seen his sister wear a bracelet which
he knew was one that had been given to Dolores
by Colonel Starbottle. That Miss Jo would n't
say where she got it, but owned up to having seen
Culpepper that day. Then the most cur'o's thing
of it yet, what does Culpepper do but rise up and
takes all back that he said, and allows that he *did*
give her the bracelet. Now my opinion, gentlemen, is that he lied; it ain't like that man to give
a gal that he respects anything off of that piece,
Dolores. But it's all the same now, and there's
but one thing to be done."

The way this one thing was done belongs to the
record of Madroño Hollow. The morning was
bright and clear; the air was slightly chill, but
that was from the mist which arose along the banks
of the river. As early as six o'clock the desig-
nated ground — a little opening in the madroño
grove — was occupied by Culpepper Starbottle,
Colonel Starbottle, his second, and the surgeon.
The Colonel was exalted and excited, albeit in a

rather imposing, dignified way, and pointed out to the surgeon the excellence of the ground, which at that hour was wholly shaded from the sun, whose steady stare is more or less discomposing to your duellist. The surgeon threw himself on the grass and smoked his cigar. Culpepper, quiet and thoughtful, leaned against a tree and gazed up the river. There was a strange suggestion of a picnic about the group, which was heightened when the Colonel drew a bottle from his coat-tails, and, taking a preliminary draught, offered it to the others. "Cocktails, sir," he explained with dignified precision. "A gentleman, sir, should never go out without 'em. Keeps off the morning chill. I remember going out in '53 with Hank Boompirater. Good ged, sir, the man had to put on his overcoat, and was shot in it. Fact."

But the noise of wheels drowned the Colonel's reminiscences, and a rapidly driven buggy, containing Jack Folinsbee, Calhoun Bungstarter, his second, and Bill Masters, drew up on the ground. Jack Folinsbee leaped out gayly. "I had the jolliest work to get away without the governor's hearing," he began, addressing the group before him with the greatest volubility. Calhoun Bungstarter touched his arm, and the young man blushed. It was his first duel.

"If you are ready, gentlemen," said Mr. Bungstarter, "we had better proceed to business. I believe it is understood that no apology will be offered or accepted. We may as well settle preliminaries at once, or I fear we shall be interrupted. There is a rumor in town that the Vigilance Committee are seeking our friends the Starbottles, and I believe, as their fellow-countryman, I have the honor to be included in their warrant."

At this probability of interruption, that gravity which had hitherto been wanting fell upon the group. The preliminaries were soon arranged and the principals placed in position. Then there was a silence.

To a spectator from the hill, impressed with the picnic suggestion, what might have been the popping of two champagne corks broke the stillness.

Culpepper had fired in the air. Colonel Starbottle uttered a low curse. Jack Folinsbee sulkily demanded another shot.

Again the parties stood opposed to each other. Again the word was given, and what seemed to be the simultaneous report of both pistols rose upon the air. But after an interval of a few seconds all were surprised to see Culpepper slowly raise his unexploded weapon and fire it harmlessly above his head. Then, throwing the pistol upon the ground, he walked to a tree and leaned silently against it.

Jack Folinsbee flew into a paroxysm of fury. Colonel Starbottle raved and swore. Mr. Bungstarter was properly shocked at their conduct. "Really, gentlemen, if Mr. Culpepper Starbottle declines another shot, I do not see how we can proceed."

But the Colonel's blood was up, and Jack Folinsbee was equally implacable. A hurried consultation ensued, which ended by Colonel Starbottle taking his nephew's place as principal, Bill Masters acting as second, *vice* Mr. Bungstarter, who declined all further connection with the affair.

Two distinct reports rang through the Hollow. Jack Folinsbee dropped his smoking pistol, took a step forward, and then dropped heavily upon his face.

In a moment the surgeon was at his side. The confusion was heightened by the trampling of hoofs, and the voice of the blacksmith bidding them flee for their lives before the coming storm. A moment more and the ground was cleared, and the surgeon, looking up, beheld only the white face of Culpepper bending over him.

"Can you save him ?"

"I cannot say. Hold up his head a moment, while I run to the buggy."

Culpepper passed his arm tenderly around the neck of the insensible man. Presently the surgeon returned with some stimulants.

"There, that will do, Mr. Starbottle, thank you. Now my advice is to get away from here while you can. I 'll look after Folinsbee. Do you hear ? "

Culpepper's arm was still round the neck of his late foe, but his head had drooped and fallen on the wounded man's shoulder. The surgeon looked down, and, catching sight of his face, stooped and lifted him gently in his arms. He opened his coat and waistcoat. There was blood upon his shirt, and a bullet-hole in his breast. He had been shot unto death at the first fire.

THE POET OF SIERRA FLAT.

A S the enterprising editor of the "Sierra Flat
Record" stood at his case setting type for
his next week's paper, he could not help hearing
the woodpeckers who were busy on the roof above
his head. It occurred to him that possibly the
birds had not yet learned to recognize in the rude
structure any improvement on nature, and this idea
pleased him so much that he incorporated it in the
editorial article which he was then doubly compos-
ing. For the editor was also printer of the "Record"; and although that remarkable journal was
reputed to exert a power felt through all Calaveras and a greater part of Tuolumne County, strict
economy was one of the conditions of its beneficent
existence.

Thus preoccupied, he was startled by the sudden
irruption of a small roll of manuscript, which was
thrown through the open door and fell at his feet.
He walked quickly to the threshold and looked
down the tangled trail which led to the high-road.
But there was nothing to suggest the presence of
his mysterious contributor. A hare limped slowly
away, a green-and-gold lizard paused upon a pine

stump, the woodpeckers ceased their work. So complete had been his sylvan seclusion, that he found it difficult to connect any human agency with the act; rather the hare seemed to have an inexpressibly guilty look, the woodpeckers to maintain a significant silence, and the lizard to be conscience-stricken into stone.

An examination of the manuscript, however, corrected this injustice to defenceless nature. It was evidently of human origin, — being verse, and of exceeding bad quality. The editor laid it aside. As he did so he thought he saw a face at the window. Sallying out in some indignation, he penetrated the surrounding thicket in every direction, but his search was as fruitless as before. The poet, if it were he, was gone.

A few days after this the editorial seclusion was invaded by voices of alternate expostulation and entreaty. Stepping to the door, the editor was amazed at beholding Mr. Morgan McCorkle, a well-known citizen of Angelo, and a subscriber to the " Record," in the act of urging, partly by force and partly by argument, an awkward young man toward the building. When he had finally effected his object, and, as it were, safely landed his prize in a chair, Mr. McCorkle took off his hat, carefully wiped the narrow isthmus of forehead which divided his black brows from his stubby hair, and with an explanatory wave of his hand toward his

reluctant companion, said, " A borned poet, and the
cussedest fool you ever seed ! "

Accepting the editor's smile as a recognition of
the introduction, Mr. McCorkle panted and went
on : " Did n't want to come ! ' Mister Editor don't
want to see me, Morg,' sez he. ' Milt,' sez I, ' he
do ; a borned poet like you and a gifted genius like
he oughter come together sociable ! ' And I fetched
him. Ah, will yer ? " The born poet had, after
exhibiting signs of great distress, started to run.
But Mr. McCorkle was down upon him instantly,
seizing him by his long linen coat, and settled him
back in his chair. " 'T ain't no use stampeding.
Yer ye are and yer ye stays. For yer a borned
poet, — ef ye are as shy as a jackass rabbit. Look
at 'im now ! "

He certainly was not an attractive picture.
There was hardly a notable feature in his weak
face, except his eyes, which were moist and shy
and not unlike the animal to which Mr. McCorkle
had compared him. It was the face that the
editor had seen at the window.

" Knowed him for fower year, — since he war a
boy," continued Mr. McCorkle in a loud whisper.
" Allers the same, bless you ! Can jerk a rhyme as
easy as turnin' jack. Never had any eddication ;
lived out in Missooray all his life. But he 's chock
full o' poetry. On'y this mornin' sez I to him, —
he camps along o' me, — ' Milt ! ' sez I, ' are break-

fast ready?' and he up and answers back quite peart and chipper, 'The breakfast it is ready, and the birds is singing free, and it's risin' in the dawnin' light is happiness to me!' When a man," said Mr. McCorkle, dropping his voice with deep solemnity, "gets off things like them, without any call to do it, and handlin' flapjacks over a cookstove at the same time, — that man's a borned poet."

There was an awkward pause. Mr. McCorkle beamed patronizingly on his *protégé*. The born poet looked as if he were meditating another flight, — not a metaphorical one. The editor asked if he could do anything for them.

"In course you can," responded Mr. McCorkle, "that's jest it. Milt, where's that poetry?"

The editor's countenance fell as the poet produced from his pocket a roll of manuscript. He, however, took it mechanically and glanced over it. It was evidently a duplicate of the former mysterious contribution.

The editor then spoke briefly but earnestly. I regret that I cannot recall his exact words, but it appeared that never before, in the history of the "Record," had the pressure been so great upon its columns. Matters of paramount importance, deeply affecting the material progress of Sierra, questions touching the absolute integrity of Calaveras and Tuolumne as social communities. were even now waiting expression. Weeks, nay, months, must elapse before that pressure would be removed, and the "Record" could grapple with any but the sternest of topics. Again, the editor had noticed with pain the absolute decline of poetry in the foot-hills of the Sierras. Even the works of Byron and Moore attracted no attention in Dutch Flat, and a prejudice seemed to exist against Tennyson in Grass Valley. But the editor was not without hope for the future. In the course of four or five years, when the country was settled, —

"What would be the cost to print this yer?" interrupted Mr. McCorkle, quietly.

"About fifty dollars, as an advertisement," responded the editor with cheerful alacrity.

Mr. McCorkle placed the sum in the editor's hand. "Yer see thet's what I sez to Milt, 'Milt,' sez I, 'pay as you go, for you are a borned poet. Hevin no call to write, but doin' it free and spontaneous like, in course you pays. Thet's why Mr. Editor never printed your poetry.'"

"What name shall I put to it?" asked the editor.

"Milton."

It was the first word that the born poet had spoken during the interview, and his voice was so very sweet and musical that the editor looked at him curiously, and wondered if he had a sister.

"Milton : is that all?"

"Thet 's his furst name," exclaimed Mr. Mc-Corkle.

The editor here suggested that as there had been another poet of that name —

"Milt might be took for him! Thet 's bad," reflected Mr. McCorkle with simple gravity. "Well, put down his hull name, — Milton Chub-buck."

The editor made a note of the fact. "I 'll set it up now," he said. This was also a hint that the interview was ended. The poet and patron, arm in arm, drew towards the door. "In next week's paper," said the editor, smilingly, in answer to the childlike look of inquiry in the eyes of the poet, and in another moment they were gone.

The editor was as good as his word. He straight-way betook himself to his case, and, unrolling the manuscript, began his task. The woodpeckers on the roof recommenced theirs, and in a few moments the former sylvan seclusion was restored. There was no sound in the barren, barn-like room but the birds above, and below the click of the composing-rule as the editor marshalled the types into lines in his stick, and arrayed them in solid column on the galley. Whatever might have been his opinion of the copy before him, there was no indication of it in his face, which wore the stolid indifference of his craft. Perhaps this was unfortunate, for as the day wore on and the level rays of the sun began

to pierce the adjacent thicket, they sought out and
discovered an anxious ambushed figure drawn up
beside the editor's window, — a figure that had sat
there motionless for hours.   Within, the editor
worked on as steadily and impassively as Fate.
And without, the born poet of Sierra Flat sat and
watched him as waiting its decree.

The effect of the poem on Sierra Flat was remarkable and unprecedented.   The absolute vile-
ness of its doggerel, the gratuitous imbecility of
its thought, and above all the crowning audacity
of the fact that it was the work of a citizen and
published in the county paper, brought it instantly
into popularity.   For many months Calaveras had
languished for a sensation ; since the last vigilance
committee nothing had transpired to dispel the
listless *ennui* begotten of stagnant business and
growing civilization.   In more prosperous moments the office of the " Record " would have been
simply gutted and the editor deported ; at present
the paper was in such demand that the edition
was speedily exhausted.   In brief, the poem of
Mr. Milton Chubbuck came like a special providence to Sierra Flat.   It was read by camp-fires,
in lonely cabins, in flaring bar-rooms and noisy
saloons, and declaimed from the boxes of stage-
coaches.   It was sung in Poker Flat with the ad-
dition of a local chorus, and danced as an unhal-

lowed rhythmic dance by the Pyrrhic phalanx of
One Horse Gulch, known as "The Festive Stags
of Calaveras." Some unhappy ambiguities of expression gave rise to many new readings, notes,
and commentaries, which, I regret to state, were
more often marked by ingenuity than delicacy of
thought or expression.

Never before did poet acquire such sudden local
reputation. From the seclusion of McCorkle's
cabin and the obscurity of culinary labors, he was
haled forth into the glowing sunshine of Fame.
The name of Chubbuck was written in letters of
chalk on unpainted walls, and carved with a pick
on the sides of tunnels. A drink known variously
as "The Chubbuck Tranquillizer," or "The Chubbuck Exalter," was dispensed at the bars. For
some weeks a rude design for a Chubbuck statue,
made up of illustrations from circus and melodeon
posters, representing the genius of Calaveras in
brief skirts on a flying steed in the act of crowning the poet Chubbuck, was visible at Keeler's
Ferry. The poet himself was overborne with in-
vitations to drink and extravagant congratulations.
The meeting between Colonel Starbottle of Siskyion and Chubbuck, as previously arranged by our
"Boston," late of Roaring Camp, is said to have
been indescribably affecting. The Colonel em-
braced him unsteadily. "I could not return to
my constituents at Siskyion, sir, if this hand,

which has grasped that of the gifted Prentice and
the lamented Poe, should not have been honored
by the touch of the godlike Chubbuck. Gentlemen, American literature is looking up. Thank
you, I will take sugar in mine." It was "Boston"
who indited letters of congratulations from H. W.
Longfellow, Tennyson, and Browning, to Mr. Chubbuck, deposited them in the Sierra Flat post-office,
and obligingly consented to dictate the replies.

The simple faith and unaffected delight with
which these manifestations were received by the
poet and his patron might have touched the hearts
of these grim masters of irony, but for the sudden
and equal development in both of the variety of
weak natures. Mr. McCorkle basked in the popularity of his *protégé*, and became alternately super-
cilious or patronizing toward the dwellers of Sierra
Flat; while the poet, with hair carefully oiled and
curled, and bedecked with cheap jewelry and
flaunting neck-handkerchief, paraded himself before the single hotel. As may be imagined, this
new disclosure of weakness afforded intense satisfaction to Sierra Flat, gave another lease of popularity to the poet, and suggested another idea to
the facetious "Boston."

At that time a young lady popularly and pro-
fessionally known as the "California Pet" was per-
forming to enthusiastic audiences in the interior.
Her specialty lay in the personation of youthful

masculine character; as a *gamin* of the street she
was irresistible, as a negro-dancer she carried the
honest miner's heart by storm. A saucy, pretty
brunette, she had preserved a wonderful moral
reputation even under the Jove-like advances of
showers of gold that greeted her appearance on
the stage at Sierra Flat. A prominent and delighted member of that audience was Milton Chubbuck. He attended every night. Every day he
lingered at the door of the Union Hotel for a
glimpse of the "California Pet." It was not long
before he received a note from her, — in "Boston's" most popular and approved female hand, —
acknowledging his admiration. It was not long
before "Boston" was called upon to indite a suitable reply. At last, in furtherance of his facetious
design, it became necessary for "Boston" to call
upon the young actress herself and secure her personal participation. To her he unfolded a plan,
the successful carrying out of which he felt would
secure his fame to posterity as a practical humorist. The "California Pet's" black eyes sparkled
approvingly and mischievously. She only stipu-
lated that she should see the man first, — a con-
cession to her feminine weakness which years of
dancing Juba and wearing trousers and boots had
not wholly eradicated from her wilful breast. By
all means, it should be done. And the interview
was arranged for the next week.

It must not be supposed that during this interval of popularity Mr. Chubbuck had been unmindful of his poetic qualities. A certain portion of each day he was absent from town, — "a communin' with natur'," as Mr. McCorkle expressed it, — and actually wandering in the mountain trails, or lying on his back under the trees, or gathering fragrant herbs and the bright-colored berries of the Marzanita. These and his company he generally brought to the editor's office, late in the afternoon, often to that enterprising journalist's infinite weariness. Quiet and uncommunicative, he would sit there patiently watching him at his work until the hour for closing the office arrived, when he would as quietly depart. There was something so humble and unobtrusive in these visits, that the editor could not find it in his heart to deny them, and accepting them, like the woodpeckers, as a part of his sylvan surroundings, often forgot even his presence. Once or twice, moved by some beauty of expression in the moist, shy eyes, he felt like seriously admonishing his visitor of his idle folly ; but his glance falling upon the oiled hair and the gorgeous necktie, he invariably thought better of it. The case was evidently hopeless.

The interview between Mr. Chubbuck and the "California Pet" took place in a private room of the Union Hotel ; propriety being respected by

the presence of that arch-humorist, "Boston." To
this gentleman we are indebted for the only true
account of the meeting. However reticent Mr.
Chubbuck might have been in the presence of his
own sex, toward the fairer portion of humanity he
was, like most poets, exceedingly voluble. Accustomed as the "California Pet" had been to exces-
sive compliment, she was fairly embarrassed by
the extravagant praises of her visitor. Her personation of boy characters, her dancing of the
"champion jig," were particularly dwelt upon
with fervid but unmistakable admiration. At
last, recovering her audacity and emboldened by
the presence of "Boston," the "California Pet"
electrified her hearers by demanding, half jestingly,
half viciously, if it were as a boy or a girl that she
was the subject of his flattering admiration.

"That knocked him out o' time," said the delighted "Boston," in his subsequent account of the
interview. "But do you believe the d—d fool
actually asked her to take him with her; wanted
to engage in the company."

The plan, as briefly unfolded by "Boston," was
to prevail upon Mr. Chubbuck to make his appearance in costume (already designed and prepared
by the inventor) before a Sierra Flat audience, and
recite an original poem at the Hall immediately
on the conclusion of the "California Pet's" per-
formance. At a given signal the audience were to

rise and deliver a volley of unsavory articles (previously provided by the originator of the scheme); then a select few were to rush on the stage, seize the poet, and, after marching him in triumphal procession through town, were to deposit him beyond its uttermost limits, with strict injunctions never to enter it again. To the first part of the plan the poet was committed, for the latter portion it was easy enough to find participants.

The eventful night came, and with it an audience that packed the long narrow room with one dense mass of human beings. The "California Pet" never had been so joyous, so reckless, so fascinating and audacious before. But the applause was tame and weak compared to the ironical outburst that greeted the second rising of the curtain and the entrance of the born poet of Sierra Flat. Then there was a hush of expectancy, and the poet stepped to the foot-lights and stood with his manuscript in his hand.

His face was deadly pale. Either there was some suggestion of his fate in the faces of his audience, or some mysterious instinct told him of his danger. He attempted to speak, but faltered, tottered, and staggered to the wings.

Fearful of losing his prey, "Boston" gave the signal and leaped upon the stage. But at the same moment a light figure darted from behind the scenes, and delivering a kick that sent the discomfited humorist back among the musicians, cut a pigeon-wing, executed a double-shuffle, and then advancing to the foot-lights with that inimitable look, that audacious swagger and utter *abandon* which had so thrilled and fascinated them a moment before, uttered the characteristic speech: " Wot are you goin' to hit a man fur, when he 's down, s-a-a-y ? "

The look, the drawl, the action, the readiness, and above all the downright courage of the little woman, had its effect. A roar of sympathetic applause followed the act. " Cut and run while you can," she whispered hurriedly over her one shoulder, without altering the other's attitude of pert and saucy defiance toward the audience. But even as she spoke the poet tottered and sank fainting upon the stage. Then she threw a despairing whisper behind the scenes, " Ring down the curtain."

There was a slight movement of opposition in the audience, but among them rose the burly shoulders of Yuba Bill, the tall, erect figure of Henry York of Sandy Bar, and the colorless, determined face of John Oakhurst. The curtain came down.

Behind it knelt the " California Pet " beside the prostrate poet. " Bring me some water. Run for a doctor. Stop !! CLEAR OUT, ALL OF YOU ! "

She had unloosed the gaudy cravat and opened

the shirt-collar of the insensible figure before her.
Then she burst into an hysterical laugh.

" Manuela ! "

Her tiring-woman, a Mexican half-breed, came
toward her.

" Help me with him to my dressing-room, quick ;
then stand outside and wait. If any one questions you, tell them he 's gone. Do you hear ?
HE 's gone."

The old woman did as she was bade. In a few
moments the audience had departed. Before morning so also had the " California Pet," Manuela, and
— the poet of Sierra Flat.

But, alas ! with them also had departed the fair
fame of the " California Pet." Only a few, and
these it is to be feared of not the best moral character themselves, still had faith in the stainless
honor of their favorite actress. " It was a mighty
foolish thing to do, but it 'll all come out right
yet." On the other hand, a majority gave her
full credit and approbation for her undoubted pluck
and gallantry, but deplored that she should have
thrown it away upon a worthless object. To elect
for a lover the despised and ridiculed vagrant of
Sierra Flat, who had not even the manliness to
stand up in his own defence, was not only evidence
of inherent moral depravity, but was an insult to
the community. Colonel Starbottle saw in it only
another instance of the extreme frailty of the sex ;

he had known similar cases; and remembered distinctly, sir, how a well-known Philadelphia heiress, one of the finest women that ever rode in her kerridge, that, gad, sir! had thrown over a Southern member of Congress to consort with a d—d nigger. The Colonel had also noticed a singular look in the dog's eye which he did not entirely fancy. He would not say anything against the lady, sir, but he had noticed — And here haply the Colonel became so mysterious and darkly confidential as to be unintelligible and inaudible to the bystanders.

A few days after the disappearance of Mr. Chubbuck a singular report reached Sierra Flat, and it was noticed that "Boston," who since the failure of his elaborate joke had been even more depressed in spirits than is habitual with great humorists, suddenly found that his presence was required in San Francisco. But as yet nothing but the vaguest surmises were afloat, and nothing definite was known.

It was a pleasant afternoon when the editor of the "Sierra Flat Record" looked up from his case and beheld the figure of Mr. Morgan McCorkle standing in the doorway. There was a distressed look on the face of that worthy gentleman that at once enlisted the editor's sympathizing attention. He held an open letter in his hand, as he advanced toward the middle of the room.

"As a man as has allers borne a fair reputation," began Mr. McCorkle slowly, "I should like, if so be as I could, Mister Editor, to make a correction in the columns of your valooable paper."

Mr. Editor begged him to proceed.

"Ye may not disremember that about a month ago I fetched here what so be as we'll call a young man whose name might be as it were Milton — Milton Chubbuck."

Mr. Editor remembered perfectly.

"Thet same party I'd knowed better nor fower year, two on 'em campin' out together. Not that I'd known him all the time, fur he war shy and strange at spells and had odd ways that I took war nat'ral to a borned poet. Ye may remember that I said he was a borned poet?"

The editor distinctly did.

"I picked this same party up in St. Jo., takin' a fancy to his face, and kinder calklating he'd runn'd away from home, — for I'm a married man, Mr. Editor, and hev children of my own, — and thinkin' belike he was a borned poet."

"Well?" said the editor.

"And as I said before, I should like now to make a correction in the columns of your valooable paper."

"What correction?" asked the editor.

"I said, ef you remember my words, as how he was a borned poet."

"Yes."

"From statements in this yer letter it seems as how I war wrong."

"Well ?"

"She war a woman."

THE CHRISTMAS GIFT THAT CAME TO RUPERT.

A STORY FOR LITTLE SOLDIERS.

IT was the Christmas season in California, — a season of falling rain and springing grasses. There were intervals when, through driving clouds and flying scud, the sun visited the haggard hills with a miracle, and death and resurrection were as one, and out of the very throes of decay a joyous life struggled outward and upward. Even the storms that swept down the dead leaves nurtured the tender buds that took their places. There were no episodes of snowy silence ; over the quickening fields the farmer's ploughshare hard followed the furrows left by the latest rains. Perhaps it was for this reason that the Christmas evergreens which decorated the drawing-room took upon themselves a foreign aspect, and offered a weird contrast to the roses, seen dimly through the windows, as the southwest wind beat their soft faces against the panes.

"Now," said the Doctor, drawing his chair closer to the fire, and looking mildly but firmly at

the semicircle of flaxen heads around him, " I
want it distinctly understood before I begin my
story, that I am not to be interrupted by any ridiculous questions. At the first one I shall stop.
At the second, I shall feel it my duty to adminis-
ter a dose of castor-oil, all around. The boy that
moves his legs or arms will be understood to invite
amputation. I have brought my instruments with
me, and never allow pleasure to interfere with my
business. Do you promise ? "

" Yes, sir," said six small voices, simultaneously.
The volley was, however, followed by half a dozen
dropping questions.

" Silence ! Bob, put your feet down, and stop
rattling that sword. Flora shall sit by my side,
like a little lady, and be an example to the rest.
Fung Tang shall stay, too, if he likes. Now, turn
down the gas a little ; there, that will do, — just
enough to make the fire look brighter, and to show
off the Christmas candles. Silence, everybody !
The boy who cracks an almond, or breathes too
loud over his raisins, will be put out of the room."

There was a profound silence. Bob laid his
sword tenderly aside, and nursed his leg thoughtfully. Flora, after coquettishly adjusting the
pocket of her little apron, put her arm upon the
Doctor's shoulder, and permitted herself to be
drawn beside him. Fung Tang, the little heathen
page, who was permitted, on this rare occasion, to

share the Christian revels in the drawing-room, surveyed the group with a smile that was at once sweet and philosophical. The light ticking of a French clock on the mantel, supported by a young shepherdess of bronze complexion and great symmetry of limb, was the only sound that disturbed the Christmas-like peace of the apartment, — a peace which held the odors of evergreens, new toys, cedar-boxes, glue, and varnish in an harmonious combination that passed all understanding.

" About four years ago at this time," began the Doctor, " I attended a course of lectures in a certain city. One of the professors, who was a sociable, kindly man, — though somewhat practical and hard-headed, — invited me to his house on Christmas night. I was very glad to go, as I was anxious to see one of his sons, who, though only twelve years old, was said to be very clever. I dare not tell you how many Latin verses this little fellow could recite, or how many English ones he had composed. In the first place, you 'd want me to repeat them; secondly, I 'm not a judge of poetry, Latin or English. But there were judges who said they were wonderful for a boy, and everybody predicted a splendid future for him. Everybody but his father. He shook his head doubtingly, whenever it was mentioned, for, as I have told you, he was a practical, matter-of-fact man.

"There was a pleasant party at the Professor's that night. All the children of the neighborhood were there, and among them the Professor's clever son, Rupert, as they called him, — a thin little chap, about as tall as Bobby there, and as fair and delicate as Flora by my side. His health was feeble, his father said; he seldom ran about and played with other boys, preferring to stay at home and brood over his books, and compose what he called his verses.

"Well, we had a Christmas-tree just like this, and we had been laughing and talking, calling off the names of the children who had presents on the tree, and everybody was very happy and joyous, when one of the children suddenly uttered a cry of mingled surprise and hilarity, and said, 'Here's something for Rupert; and what do you think it is?'

"We all guessed. 'A desk'; 'A copy of Milton'; 'A gold pen'; 'A rhyming dictionary.' 'No? what then?'

"'A drum!'

"'A what?' asked everybody.

"'A drum! with Rupert's name on it.'

"Sure enough there it was. A good-sized, bright, new, brass-bound drum, with a slip of paper on it, with the inscription, 'FOR RUPERT.'

"Of course we all laughed, and thought it a good joke. 'You see you're to make a noise in the world, Rupert!' said one. 'Here's parchment for the poet,' said another. 'Rupert's last work in sheepskin covers,' said a third. 'Give us a classical tune, Rupert,' said a fourth; and so on. But Rupert seemed too mortified to speak; he changed color, bit his lips, and finally burst into a passionate fit of crying, and left the room. Then those who had joked him felt ashamed, and everybody began to ask who had put the drum there. But no one knew, or if they did, the unexpected sympathy awakened for the sensitive boy kept them silent. Even the servants were called up and questioned, but no one could give any idea where it came from. And, what was still more singular, everybody declared that up to the moment it was produced, no one had seen it hanging on the tree. What do I think? Well, I have my own opinion. But no questions! Enough for you to know that Rupert did not come down stairs again that night, and the party soon after broke up.

"I had almost forgotten those things, for the war of the Rebellion broke out the next spring, and I was appointed surgeon in one of the new regiments, and was on my way to the seat of war. But I had to pass through the city where the Professor lived, and there I met him. My first question was about Rupert. The Professor shook his head sadly. 'He's not so well,' he said; 'he has been declining since last Christmas, when you saw him. A very strange case,' he added, giving it a long Latin name, — ' a very singular case. But go and see him yourself,' he urged; ' it may distract his mind and do him good.'

"I went accordingly to the Professor's house, and found Rupert lying on a sofa, propped up with pillows. Around him were scattered his books, and, what seemed in singular contrast, that drum I told you about was hanging on a nail, just above his head. His face was thin and wasted; there was a red spot on either cheek, and his eyes were very bright and widely opened. He was glad to see me, and when I told him where I was going, he asked a thousand questions about the war. I thought I had thoroughly diverted his mind from its sick and languid fancies, when he suddenly grasped my hand and drew me toward him.

"'Doctor,' said he, in a low whisper, 'you won't laugh at me if I tell you something?'

"'No, certainly not,' I said.

"'You remember that drum?' he said, pointing to the glittering toy that hung against the wall. 'You know, too, how it came to me. A few weeks after Christmas, I was lying half asleep here, and the drum was hanging on the wall, when suddenly I heard it beaten; at first, low and slowly, then faster and louder, until its rolling filled the house. In the middle of the night, I heard it again. I did not dare to tell anybody about it, but I have heard it every night ever since.'

"He paused and looked anxiously in my face. Sometimes,' he continued, 'it is played softly, ,sometimes loudly, but always quickening to a long-roll, so loud and alarming that I have looked to see people coming into my room to ask what was the matter. But I think, Doctor, — I think,' he repeated slowly, looking up with painful interest into my face, 'that no one hears it but myself.'

"I thought so, too, but I asked him if he had heard it at any other time.

"'Once or twice in the daytime,' he replied, 'when I have been reading or writing ; then very loudly, as though it were angry, and tried in that way to attract my attention away from my books.'

"I looked into his face, and placed my hand upon his pulse. His eyes were very bright, and his pulse a little flurried and quick. I then tried to explain to him that he was very weak, and that his senses were very acute, as most weak people's are ; and how that when he read, or grew interested and excited, or when he was tired at night, the throbbing of a big artery made the beating sound he heard. He listened to me with a sad smile of unbelief, but thanked me, and in a little while I went away. But as I was going down stairs, I met the Professor. I gave him my opinion of the case, — well, no matter what it was.

"'He wants fresh air and exercise,' said the Professor, 'and some practical experience of life, sir.' The Professor was not a bad man, but he was a little worried and impatient, and thought — as clever people are apt to think — that things which he did n't understand were either silly or improper.

"I left the city that very day, and in the excitement of battle-fields and hospitals, I forgot all about little Rupert, nor did I hear of him again, until one day, meeting an old classmate in the army, who had known the Professor, he told me that Rupert had become quite insane, and that in one of his paroxysms he had escaped from the house, and as he had never been found, it was feared that he had fallen in the river and was drowned. I was terribly shocked for the moment, as you may imagine; but, dear me, I was living just then among scenes as terrible and shocking, and I had little time to spare to mourn over poor Rupert.

"It was not long after receiving this intelligence that we had a terrible battle, in which a portion of our army was surprised and driven back with great slaughter. I was detached from my brigade to ride over to the battle-field and assist the surgeons of the beaten division, who had more on their hands than they could attend to. When I reached the barn that served for a temporary hospital, I went at once to work. Ah, Bob," said the Doctor, thoughtfully taking the bright sword from the hands of the half-frightened Bob, and holding it gravely before him, "these pretty play-things are symbols of cruel, ugly realities.

"I turned to a tall, stout Vermonter," he con-tinued very slowly, tracing a pattern on the rug with the point of the scabbard, "who was badly wounded in both thighs, but he held up his hands and begged me to help others first who needed it more than he. I did not at first heed his request, for this kind of unselfishness was very common in the army; but he went on, 'For God's sake, Doc-tor, leave me here; there is a drummer-boy of our regiment — a mere child — dying, if he is n't dead now. Go, and see him first. He lies over there. He saved more than one life. He was at his post in the panic this morning, and saved the honor of the regiment.' I was so much more impressed by the man's manner than by the substance of his speech, which was, however, corroborated by the other poor fellows stretched around me, that I passed over to where the drummer lay, with his drum beside him. I gave one glance at his face —and — yes, Bob — yes, my children — it *was* Rupert.

"Well! well! it needed not the chalked cross which my brother-surgeons had left upon the rough board whereon he lay to show how urgent was the relief he sought; it needed not the prophetic words of the Vermonter, nor the damp that mingled with the brown curls that clung to his pale forehead, to show how hopeless it was now. I called him by name. He opened his eyes — larger, I thought, in the new vision that was beginning to dawn upon him — and recognized me. He whispered, 'I'm glad you are come, but I don't think you can do me any good.'

"I could not tell him a lie. I could not say anything. I only pressed his hand in mine, as he went on.

"'But you will see father, and ask him to forgive me. Nobody is to blame but myself. It was a long time before I understood why the drum came to me that Christmas night, and why it kept calling to me every night, and what it said. I know it now. The work is done, and I am content. Tell father it is better as it is. I should have lived only to worry and perplex him, and something in me tells me this is right.'

"He lay still for a moment, and then, grasping my hand, said, —

"'Hark!'

"I listened, but heard nothing but the suppressed moans of the wounded men around me. 'The drum,' he said faintly; 'don't you hear it? The drum is calling me.'

"He reached out his arm to where it lay, as though he would embrace it.

"'Listen,' he went on, 'it's the reveille. There are the ranks drawn up in review. Don't you see the sunlight flash down the long line of bayonets? Their faces are shining, — they present arms, — there comes the General; but his face I cannot look at, for the glory round his head. He sees me; he smiles, it is —' And with a name upon his lips that he had learned long ago, he stretched himself wearily upon the planks, and lay quite still.

"That's all. No questions now; never mind what became of the drum. Who's that snivelling? Bless my soul, where's my pill-box?"